"You Don't Know A Lot Of Things About Me, Glory,"

Bill replied. "But eventually, I'm afraid you and everyone else in this town are going to find out much more than you ever cared to."

"You said before that I had hardly changed, well I'm not the same girl you left behind," Glory stated defensively. "For one thing I've learned not to involve myself in matters that are none of my business."

Bill smiled mockingly. "There was a time when everything I did was your business."

"It used to be that I gave two hoots about you," she reminded him with saccharine sweetness. "But I was very young then, and very foolish."

"Very young and very beautiful," he corrected, using the low, caressing tone of voice that she'd never been able to forget. "And very desirable..."

Dear Reader:

Spring is in the air! Birds are singing, flowers are blooming and thoughts are turning to love. Since springtime is such a romantic time, I'm happy to say that April's Silhouette Desires are the very essence of romance.

Now we didn't exactly plan it this way, but three of our books this month are connecting stories. *The Hidden Pearl* by Celeste Hamilton is part of **Aunt Eugenia's Treasures**. *Ladies' Man* by Raye Morgan ties into *Husband for Hire* (#434). And our *Man of the Month*, Garret Cagan in Ann Major's *Scandal's Child* ties into her successful **Children of Destiny** series.

I know many of you love connecting stories, but if you haven't read the "prequels" and spin-offs, please remember that each and every Silhouette Desire is a wonderful love story in its own right.

And don't miss our other April books: *King of the Mountain* by Joyce Thies, *Guilty Secrets* by Laura Leone and *Sunshine* by Jo Ann Algermissen!

Before I go, I have to say that I'd love to know what you think about our new covers. Please write in and let me know. I'm always curious about what the readers think—and I also believe that your thoughts are important.

Until next month,

Lucia Macro
Senior Editor

JOYCE
THIES

KING OF THE MOUNTAIN

SILHOUETTE *Desire*

Published by Silhouette Books New York

America's Publisher of Contemporary Romance

SILHOUETTE BOOKS
300 East 42nd St., New York, N.Y. 10017

ISBN: 0-373-05563-3

First Silhouette Books printing April 1990

Printed in the U.S.A.

JOYCE THIES

has been reading and writing romances since her teens but had to wait ten years before one was published. Since then she has authored or coauthored over twenty contemporary and historical novels. Readers might recognize her as the Joyce half of Janet Joyce. She wrote her first Silhouette Desire, *Territorial Rights*, as Melissa Scott, but is now writing under her own name.

She met her husband in college, and it was love at first sight. Joyce believes that out of sharing comes growth for both partners. She says, "Because of the loving man in my life, I've become everything I've ever wanted to be: wife, mother and writer. With each book I write, I imagine another woman lucky enough to have it all."

Prologue

The summer he turned six, the boy found himself a hideout down by the peatbog on the far side of McCann Mountain. It was the best hideout ever, for in the three years since, nobody, not even Big Will McCann had discovered the boy's whereabouts on those days when he felt too restless to mind his manners. Trees didn't grow much near the bog, but the swamp grasses were tall enough to hide in. Besides, once he got down past the old logging road, the boy couldn't hear his daddy calling out his name, no matter how loudly the man hollered. If he couldn't hear the call, the boy figured he wasn't obliged to answer, and then, just for a short while, mainly until his fear of a good switching got the better of him, he was free to be whomever he wanted and do pretty much as he liked.

Most days he would strip off his clothes first thing, spend a few minutes squishing his toes through the warm mud, then a few more seeing how big a splash he could make sloshing through the murky water surrounding the bullrushes. Part of the fun of doing that was knowing how horrified his mother would be if she'd ever seen him shuck down to his bare skin, let alone march up and down in broad daylight as bold as anything. And, if she'd ever seen him plunge headlong into the deep pool behind the moss-covered stump, her reaction would have been that much worse.

The boy knew how to swim, but his mother wouldn't consider the bog a safe place for her only child, and even if the woman lived to be a hundred, she would never comprehend a young boy's need to prove for himself the truth in the story that Davy Crockett used a hollow reed as a snorkel. Knowing this about her, the boy was always very careful to make sure that every bit of bog slime was out of his neatly trimmed black hair before he began his reluctant climb back to the big, gray stone house on the top of the mountain. In that house there was room for neither nonsense nor make-believe.

Unfortunately, he was soon to learn that his secret hiding place was no longer a secret. At first, when he heard the wild splashing, he was afraid that the older boys who'd moved into the small, white, frame house at the bottom of the mountain had discovered his swimming hole, but then he peeked through the grass and saw that his trespasser was only a girl—one, stark-naked, pint-size girl. He guessed her to be about six or seven, but she was still capable of making some very impressive splashes, and as he watched her small form glide gracefully under the water, he noted that she could also swim like a fish.

At nine, the boy was far older than his years, but even if he hadn't been, he'd long since been taught that most folks would consider it sinful for him to be spying on her. He probably should have felt guilty, but he didn't. With her petite body, fair white skin, curly red hair and big blue eyes, she was the prettiest little thing he'd ever laid eyes on, and he was fascinated by her playful antics in the water.

The longer he watched her the more she reminded him of the innocent-looking pink-and-white flowers that grew along the edges of the marsh, but that comparison made him even more wary of discovery. He knew what happened to the foolhardy insects that were drawn to those beautiful clusters of sundew. One minute they were free to fly, and the next they were trapped in the enticing dewdrops that clung to the delicate red hairs of each leafy rosette. Because of his mother, the boy could easily identify with the hopeless feeling, and he'd also developed a strong mistrust of feminine beauty.

The little girl he was watching was very pretty on the outside, but the boy had learned early on that a sweet face could mask a cold nature. Beyond that suspicion, he had the strange notion that if he took the risk of confronting her, the child just might reach out to capture something deep down inside him and make it impossible for him to escape. Avoiding snares, especially the kind that grown-ups liked to set for him, was one of the boy's greatest talents.

Deciding that he could be in danger of springing a different but equally risky kind of trap with this particular interloper, he took a step backward, but then he heard her laughter and it stopped him in his tracks. Never in his life had he heard a person, young or old, laugh so clearly out of pure joy. Hearing it, he had to question his unkind suspicions. What if she really was just as sweet as she appeared?

Seconds later, he discovered that the child had extremely acute hearing and had yet to be taught that nakedness was shameful. Just as feisty as you please, she stood up in the shallow water, placed her hands on her hips and stared straight at his hiding place. "Ain't you coming in?" The boy cleared his throat and took a tentative step out onto the muddy bank, still uncertain of his welcome. "I was," he admitted reluctantly. "But I figured I'd scare you."

The child's delighted laughter reminded him of the bubbly water that tumbled over the polished stones in Hickory Creek. "Why should I be afeared of the likes of you? You ain't so big and not nearly so mean and ornery as folks say."

"Is that so? And how would you know that, L'il Bit?"

Eyes as bright blue as the summer sky focused intently on his face and the boy had the uncomfortable feeling that they could see clean inside his skin. "I come here purty regular to watch your play actin'," she informed him smugly. "But sometimes your pretendin' don't help none. Sometimes you're real sad and lonesome and you cry. I decided to come play with you today, so's you won't cry no more."

Both embarrassed and angered by her unexpected knowledge of his secret weakness, the boy blustered, "What I do here is none of your business!"

Frowning fiercely at him, the child said, "I can care about you iffen I want to!"

Amazed by her attitude as much as her words, the boy retorted, "Why the heck should you?"

With a long-suffering sigh, the child repeated what her Aunt Carrie Hubbard often said when describing her. "I'm afeared it's my lot in life to care for hurtin' things cuz they always pain me so. Right here."

She curled one small hand over her heart, and the boy felt a sudden tightness in his own chest. "Well, I don't need any namby-pamby girl caring for me!" he insisted belligerently. "So get out of here before I set the dogs on ya'. You're trespassin' on private property!"

Ignoring his warning, the child smiled beguilingly, her gaze gentle as she held out her hand to him. "I know this is rightly your very own special place, Billy D. Still, I didn't figure you'd mind sharing it with a friend."

The boy's mouth dropped open in amazement. He wasn't allowed friends, at least not ones of his own choosing, and no one had ever called him by a nickname. No one would have dared, but this bright-eyed little girl didn't seem the least bit fearful of offending her betters. "Why did you call me that?" he asked curiously, for there was no need to question how she knew who he was. His parents made sure that every person in Jessup County knew that.

The child gave him a look of such compassion that the boy flushed. "My Aunt Winnie Hubbard says true friends be callin' each other by friendly names. That's why you can call me Glory. L'il Bit was nice, too, but soon I'll be all growed," she declared seriously. "And it won't sound so nice no more."

"No, I guess it wouldn't," the boy conceded, fighting to keep a straight face. It would be years and years before this tiny sprite was "all growed," but she would be crushed if he told her that, and for reasons he didn't understand, he couldn't bring himself to hurt her feelings. "And your Aunt's right. Friends should be friendly, so Glory it'll be."

Gratified by his acceptance of her logic, the child nodded, but then her eyes lit up with an impish sparkle. Quick as a flash, she scooped some water into her hands and doused his shirtfront. The next second, she was gone, diving into deeper water. Open-mouthed, the boy stared down at his wet shirt, then up again as he heard the joyful trill of her laughter accompanied by a lilting song. "Poor Billy D., he can't get me. Can't get me. Can't get me."

"Wanna bet?" the boy challenged while he struggled with the unaccustomed need to match her nonsensical rhyme. He was stripped all the way down to his socks before he thought of one. "You're going to be sorry, little Glory," he called out, laughing gleefully as he plunged into the water after her.

At the edge of the pool, a buzzing deerfly was attracted to the bright red filaments of the flower. Sensing danger, its powerful wings lifted higher, but it was already too late. The insect was captured and held fast by the glistening dewdrops that sparkled in the sunlight.

One

For the past thirty years, the McCann Lumber Company had sponsored a picnic that was held in the town square each Fourth of July. This year the picnic went off right on schedule, but with one major difference. The owner of the company wasn't strolling around the crowded pavilion making speeches, kissing babies and shaking hands. Big Will McCann, Hillsborough, West Virginia's most influential citizen, had finally succumbed to the liver disease brought on by his years of hard drinking.

Many mourned his passing, but not because of any great love they'd felt for the man. Without Big Will manning the helm, it was feared that his company would either be sold or go under, and without McCann Lumber, there would be no town.

Normally, the annual event was a festive occasion, but not this year. As all in attendance waited for the announcement that would determine their future ability to put food on their tables, the atmosphere inside the pavilion grew increasingly somber. Since the decision to close or stay open was going to be made by Big Will's son, a man whom no one had seen or heard from in close to ten years, the anxiety level was running high. William Daniel McCann II was a stranger to them, and few among them believed that a stranger could be trusted.

However, one group at the gathering hadn't resigned themselves to whatever decree this prodigal son felt inclined to hand down to them. With three members of their family counting on the company for employment, the Hubbard sisters felt it was their duty to influence the man in the proper direction. Of course, since he'd been a young boy when they'd last had any close dealings with him, he might not remember what they were about, but most folks in Hillsborough were well aware that when the Hubbard sisters had an opinion to offer, they offered it, whether it was appreciated or not. Pride Goeth Before a Fall was their sisterly motto, and they paid absolutely no heed to those who didn't abide by that doctrine.

"As I always say, the apple never falls too far from the tree," Carrie Hubbard said, introducing the topic needing discussion, glancing pointedly over the wire rims of her spectacles at a small, birdlike woman with clear blue eyes who was seated directly across from her at the picnic table. "I hate to speak ill of the dead, but Big Will was as hard as nails when he wanted to be, and it's beginning to look like his son has turned out just like him. Don't you agree, Winnie?"

As usual, before the more reticent Winnifred got the chance to respond to the question, Ophelia, who at seventy-five was the eldest of the three sisters by two years, answered for her. Tucking a loose strand of snowy-white hair into her tight bun, she declared, "Too true, sister, but that don't mean we cain't change his mind for him. I say somebody should step in and give him what for."

"I couldn't agree more, sister," Carrie replied. "And this picnic gives us the perfect chance. If the ornery way he's been acting since his daddy's funeral is any indication, this may be the only time he comes down off that blamed mountain. Cousin Ida May Potter says he's been spendin' all his time up there broodin' 'bout things that cain't be changed. Hasn't stepped one foot in the office or the mill. Wasn't even plannin' to attend the doin's today, until she told him how folks were carryin' on so. 'Spect he didn't want to hear that, neither."

"Ida May thinks he's gotta mind to sell out and be movin' on again," Ophelia said, shaking her head in disapproval. "Now wouldn't that be a tragedy, and not just for those workin' for the company? For all his wanderin' ways, his place is here and always has been. Not to mention that little boy of his. Why Ida May says that young'n don't have the least notion who he is or where he rightly belongs in this world."

A definite note of pleading in her soft voice, Winnifred entered the conversation for the first time. "Ain't that a blessed shame? A child needs to put down strong roots if he's to sprout up good and sturdy."

Carrie nodded gravely. "Now that's a fact, sister, and our family lends truth to the notion. We've known our fair share of tragedy, but there's nothin' a body cain't get through when he's supported by his kin."

"He might not be blood relation, but all folks in this town are kinfolk, no matter how far they might choose to wander," Ophelia declared staunchly. "That being so, I say we're honor bound to set things right, don't you, sisters? It's time that young man realized that a seed don't choose where it's planted, but takes what it needs from the soil and grows up as good as it possibly can be."

"Then it's agreed," Carrie said, smiling benignly down the table at the one member of their party who had yet to utter a single word or agree to anything. At twenty-five, Gloria Hubbard was much younger than the three other women, but her kinship to them was obvious, even if her hair had yet to change from vibrant red to their snowy white. Her eyes were the same sunny blue as theirs, and she possessed the same delicate features and fragile bone structure that had been passed down to all the female members of the Hubbard clan from one generation to the next.

At the moment, however, as she felt the hopeful gazes of all three of her maiden aunts focus meaningfully on her face, she would've gladly given up her family membership. "Not by me it isn't!" she exclaimed fiercely, and when that statement had no effect, she insisted, "I'm the very *last* person you should ask to approach him."

"Nonsense." Carrie dismissed that heated claim with a regal wave of her hand. "Since you know so much about child psychology and the like, who could be better than you to deal with the situation?"

"Anyone!" Glory persisted, but her aunts simply smiled at her, obviously rejecting her protests as completely ridiculous.

"Think of that innocent little boy of his and what his young life must have been like up till now, driftin' from one place to another like so much flotsam in a stream," Winnie suggested. "Now, Glory, you cain't tell me you think that's healthy."

Glory didn't want to think about this particular child at all, but her aunts would never approve of such an unfeeling attitude on her part, no matter what her justification. Indeed, they wouldn't believe her capable of placing her own selfish needs before that of any child. After all, they would say, hadn't she applied for that scholarship and worked so hard to earn that fancy degree in child development because she cared so much more about the welfare of children than most other folks? Why, if she hadn't taken it upon herself to apply for that complicated government grant, those poor children who attended her day-care program would still be left to their own devices while their folks labored in the mill.

Glory didn't wish to hear that lecture, any more than she wanted to listen to anything else her elderly aunts had to say on this subject. "If I'd known you three would try and put me up to something like this, I never would have come to this shindig." Beginning to think that she was the subject of a major conspiracy, she inquired, "And where, may I ask, are my dear brothers?"

"We told them to make themselves scarce until after we'd talked to you," Carrie replied matter-of-factly, glancing down at the cameo timepiece pinned to her thin bosom. "Don't worry none, they be gangin' up at Ken 'n' Liliah's place and they'll all be here as soon as we commence to eatin'."

Ophelia opened a large wicker basket and set down a huge platter of Southern-fried chicken and a basket of biscuits next to the other assorted crockery placed on the table, while her sisters arranged plates, silverware and cups on the far end. "We have great faith in you, Glory. Somehow, you'll manage to get past your personal grievances with that man and advise him to stick with what he has, cuz there ain't nothin' better somewheres else."

"You might feel more kindly toward the man if you remember what a hard day this must be for 'im," Winnifred reminded her niece gently, reaching across the red-and-white checkered tablecloth to pat her hand reassuringly.

Glory opened her mouth to say it was fast becoming an extremely hard day for her as well, but swiftly closed it again, knowing her aunts would view that remark as highly uncharitable. On the other hand, she'd often heard them advocate the philosophy that charity begins at home. Was it fair of them to involve her in a situation that had nothing whatsoever to do with her? Absolutely not, she concluded.

"Meeting up with me again will only make the day that much harder for him," she argued, struggling to keep her voice down to a reasonable level when what she really wanted to do was scream that she couldn't possibly do what they wanted, no matter what they said. There had been a time when she'd loved William Daniel McCann II with all of her heart, but he'd trampled her tender feelings into the ground, then had taken off for parts unknown.

Considering the humiliation she'd once suffered on his account, Glory would have died supremely happy if she never set eyes on him again. Indeed, if anyone in her treacherous family had seen fit to tell her that the man had stayed on well past his daddy's funeral and was going to be in attendance today, she wouldn't have come anywhere near this place. "Why you think he'd listen to anything I might have to say is beyond me!"

"As I recall, you once had a real talent for making him listen," Carrie said, sending her sisters an amused wink when Glory wasn't looking. "Especially when it came to things he didn't want to hear."

"That might have been true before his folks shipped him off to military school, but he was an entirely different person when he came back. Don't you remember how hateful he was to me that last summer he was home?" Glory complained wretchedly, hoping to inspire a little sympathy.

Unfortunately, all that question got her were some very unsympathetic chuckles. "Oh my, yes," Ophelia declared proudly. "You never did pay no mind to his being a McCann, and that riled 'im something fierce. Why, most times all you had to do was walk by 'im and those eyes of his would start glintin' dark purple, just like the nightshade that grows down by the creek."

"Well, the color of his eyes wasn't the only thing that resembled that noxious plant," Glory muttered, ignoring the fact that there'd been several times when she'd deliberately gone out of her way to incite his notorious temper. "He could spit pure poison with that smart-alecky mouth of his."

Wearing a reminiscent smile, Winnifred said, "I'll always recollect how spittin' mad he got that time you pushed him off his motorbike into the municipal fountain. He sure didn't like being made to look like a prime fool in public."

"Then he shouldn't have behaved like one," Glory retorted tartly, but as soon as she noted her aunts' approving expressions, she started back-pedaling—fast. "Thinking that and doing something about it are two different things. Considering how arrogant he was, I never should have taken such a chance in the first place, and I certainly don't intend to take any more risks where he's concerned. In my opinion, what William McCann does or doesn't do is no one's business but his own."

"Do you want to see the mill shut down for good?" Ophelia asked, her seamy face wearing the appalled expression that could always make Glory feel guilty.

"Of course not," Glory said, trying to forget that three of her brothers would be closely effected by today's decision. "But if he wants to sell out, nothing I say or do will make any difference."

Carrie apparently wasn't buying that assumption. "You stood up to 'im once, Gloria Hubbard, and we were all proud of you. You sure made him think twice about racin' that big motorbike 'round the town square, and to my recollection, he never done it again.''

Glory wished they would stop referring to that particular incident, especially when she knew that her motivation had had nothing to do with civic responsibility. She and Billy D. McCann might have been childhood friends, but after he'd returned from that elite private academy his daddy had sent him off to, he'd completely ignored her existence. Word had it that he'd been kicked out of military school for incorrigible behavior only a few months before graduation, but that hadn't mattered to any of the local girls.

At seventeen, he'd been handsome as the devil. Dressed in black leather, he'd ridden back into town on his motorcycle, the personification of all the excitement and danger that was missing from their own small-town lives. Every girl in Jessup County would have sold her soul just to be seen with him. Upon hearing what kind of sinful liberties they'd willingly allowed him to take, Glory was certain that some of them actually had. Why, after only one date with Nellie Harper, the girl had boasted that she and Billy had actually gone ''all the way.''

Unfortunately for Glory, even knowing that his years away from home had placed him way out of her league, she'd joined right in with the others in vying for his attention. She wasn't built like Nellie, but most boys found her pretty and it angered her that Billy didn't convey the slightest interest in her, especially since she felt so possessive toward him. When none of the more conventional methods had worked, she'd finally resorted to drastic measures—like pushing him into the fountain.

That action had certainly accomplished what nothing else had, Glory recalled with a grimace. Billy D. had noticed her again, all right, and that had been the beginning of a time in her life that, even after all these years, she still found extremely painful to think about.

Her aunts, however, weren't aware of the depths of her feelings toward William McCann or the reason behind her antagonism, and Glory had no intention of telling them. To her dismay, however, once they likened to an idea, the aunts would no more give up on it than a bulldog would a meaty bone. "Now, we realize you've both simmered down some since then," Ophelia allowed. "But that don't mean you still can't rile him iffen you really set your mind to it."

"But—"

"Like I've been saying," Carrie interrupted, picking up on the same theme without skipping a breath, her wrinkled brow set in determined lines. "Somebody's got to light a fire under his stubborn tail, and we figure you're just the one to do it. Whatever he thinks, he belongs here in these mountains, and so does his boy."

Even her Aunt Winnie, whom Gloria could usually count on to take her side, was nodding her head in approval of this ridiculous plan. "We've tried to talk to him our own selves, but without any luck. Why, he wouldn't accept our invitation to lunch, even when we promised to make him a sweet-potato pie. It don't seem as if he wants nothn' to do with nobody from these parts."

"I say we take the man at his word," Glory suggested, but again her words fell on deaf ears.

"It's up to you now, Glory," Carrie stated firmly. "We're all countin' on you to show him where his rightful responsibility lies."

Gloria sent a beseeching gaze skyward, sensing that nothing could save her now but divine intervention, yet determined to fight on to her last breath. "Really Aunt Carrie, I can't—"

"I see the boys comin' so you'd best start eatin' while there's still somethin' left to eat. We cain't enjoy fixin's like this every day and I aim to enjoy 'em," Ophelia decreed autocratically, effectively forestalling further argument by turning her attention to the mountain of food on her plate.

Since the first week after they'd lost their parents to influenza and been taken in by their granddaddy's three spinster sisters, the five Hubbard children—four rough 'n' tumble boys and one chatterbox little girl—had known better than to upset Great-aunt Ophelia while she was eating. The woman claimed to have a very touchy stomach and though none of them had ever witnessed any physical evidence of this malady, they knew better than to risk the onset of one of her "bile attacks." Complaints to the guilty party about the agony she'd suffered on their account had been known to drag on for several weeks.

"Boy! Did all these people really work for my grandpa?"

Bill McCann smiled at his son's wide-eyed incredulity. "Not all, Jamie, but most," he admitted, then frowned at the sudden wrench he felt in the pit of his stomach as they neared the pavilion. The last time he'd climbed those wide, painted steps and sat down on one of the folding chairs reserved for the family he'd been eighteen, and even though he was an adult now, he still hated the prospect. Jamming his hands into the front pockets of his faded jeans, he fingered the folded paper that contained his speech, reminding himself that today was the last time he would ever be required to take his proper place as a McCann.

Unaware of his father's unease, Jamie asked eagerly, "Are we related to any of them like we are to Miss Ida?"

"We aren't related to Ida," Bill replied, unable to stop his gaze from straying to the picnic table closest to the makeshift podium. If nothing had changed over the past decade, she would be there with her family.

She was. He could feel it, proving that he still had a second sense where she was concerned.

Luckily, he didn't get the chance to dwell on the fact that he would soon be seeing Gloria Eloise Hubbard again. His last comment had made six-year-old Jamie highly indignant, and unlike his father when he'd been that age, the boy felt free to state his opinions. "We are so!" he cried. "We're Ida May's shirttail kin. She told me so! She says we're still family, even if we *have* been away a long time."

Bill felt another uncomfortable twinge in his stomach, this time from guilt. "You and I are a family," Bill explained, striving for an even tone. "Shirttail kin are people who know a lot about each other, but they aren't really related. They're more like friends."

"Oh," the boy said, a wealth of disappointment in his dark eyes until he thought some more about what his father had just told him. Then he grinned. "I don't mind being shirttail, and I'm going to like having all these new friends."

"Jamie—" Bill cautioned, then stopped himself. Since birth, the boy hadn't lived in any one place long enough to form any lasting relationships, and his desire for them was perfectly natural. Unfortunately, they wouldn't be staying in Hillsborough any longer than necessary, but that didn't mean that Jamie couldn't enjoy himself to the fullest while they were here. "If things haven't changed since I used to come to these picnics, you'll find a ton of boys your age over by the dunking booth. As soon as I'm done with my speech, I'll walk you over there."

"What's a dunking booth?" Jamie asked, and Bill's explanation inspired a delighted giggle. "Boy, Dad, this town sounds pretty cool. Why don't you get yourself a job here so we can stay on awhile."

That suggestion was met by a bark of laughter from the stout, middle-aged man who stood at the bottom of the pavilion steps. "Got an openin' over at the feed store if you're interested, young Will," Caleb Bonner joked, his heavy jowls quivering with mirth as he grabbed Bill's hand in his beefy paw and began pumping it vigorously up and down. "Since I got elected mayor, I can't spend all my time behind the counter no more, but folks wouldn't mind placin' their orders with you. Course it don't pay much, but the job's yours iffen you want it."

"Thanks Mr. Bonner," Bill replied, going along with the older man's joke since that was far easier than explaining the absurdity of such an offer to his young son. As far as Jamie knew, any job offered to his father was worth fair consideration, and since the boy had no understanding of wills and inheritance laws, he assumed that they were still operating under the philosophy of a good day's wages for a good day's work.

"I'll give it some thought," he offered dryly.

"You do that," Caleb quipped, then with forced joviality, switched his attention to Jamie. "And who do we have here?"

With commendable manners, Jamie stuck out his hand. "James McCann, sir," he said, then disclosed truthfully, "but I like Jamie better, just like my dad likes Bill much better than young Will. Like I've been saying to people since we came here, he's awful old to be called young."

"So he is," Caleb acknowledged, casting a quick nervous glance at the father before he shook the child's hand. "Bill it is then, and I'm very proud to meetcha, Jamie."

"Come fall, I'll be in school all day. First grade," Jamie continued, unaware that in Hillsborough his father didn't require any extra promotion. "So if he takes the job, my Dad can put in some decent hours for you, and he's a real hard worker."

Bill saw Caleb's bushy brows lift at that amazing piece of information, but he saw no need for lengthy explanations. "As you can probably tell, Mr. Bonner, Jamie's still a bit in the dark about some things."

In the hill country, a man didn't question another man's private business, so Caleb merely nodded, but he couldn't quite hide his astonishment. Bill noted his disbelieving expression, but remained silent. Unfortunately, his son wasn't as willing to let sleeping dogs lie. "My dad's done lots of things," he boasted. "And he's good at everything he does, but he mainly likes outside jobs. Last year, he helped build a real big, long road.''

Caleb still didn't look convinced, and to prevent Jamie from giving the man a detailed history of his past employment, Bill admitted tersely, ''I worked some highway construction out of Tulsa.''

''Goodness alive!'' Caleb stroked his balding head as he led the way up the steps, as if using his hand to help his brain absorb such an unlikely prospect as Big Will and Lorraine McCann's precious only son doing manual labor. It seemed that no matter how hard he tried, the picture wouldn't come, but he was apparently wise enough not to pry any further into matters that didn't concern him.

Caleb Bonner had gotten along just fine with Big Will, but he was beginning to think that dealing with the man's son was going to be an altogether different proposition. Since he was nearing the end of his term and planned to seek reelection, Caleb couldn't afford to offend the man who now had the power to make or break both him and the community. Like everyone else in town, he knew where his bread was buttered.

With the paternal smile that had earned him a fair number of votes in the past, Caleb reached down and ruffled Jamie's hair. ''From the sounds of it, I don't reckon you've heard your daddy give too many formal speeches, have you, boy?''

''No, sir,'' Jamie admitted. ''But I'm not worried. He's got all the words written down so he won't forget what to say,'' he assured loyally.

As soon as Bill took his place on the podium, he decided that his son's confidence in him was misplaced. He wasn't nervous. What he felt was much closer to an all-out panic.

An expectant hush fell over the pavilion as Caleb introduced him to the crowd, but it wasn't a benevolent silence. The tension in the air was almost palpable, increasing the dryness in his mouth. Growing up a McCann, he'd learned to expect some animosity. As a young boy, he'd always sensed the envy and resentment other people had felt for him and his parents, although it had usually been masked behind smiling faces and pleasant words.

Today, no one was even bothering to smile.

Increasingly ill at ease, Bill took his time unfolding the paper that contained his speech, spreading it out flat before him and holding it down with one hand to keep it from blowing away. For several seconds he stared hard at the words, but even though he wanted to, he just couldn't bring himself to say them. In the lengthening silence, he gazed out over the lectern at the sea of anxious faces, some familiar, some not, and it was as if a steel clamp had snapped shut around his throat.

He tried to ignore the question, but his brain kept repeating it louder and louder. Could he honestly do this and still live with himself? Hillsborough was a company town and Big Will was the company, not him—but would anyone remember that when their paychecks stopped coming? He didn't think so, and suddenly he didn't know if he had the right to ask them to try. If he sold out, wouldn't the consequences to the community be worse than any sin his father had ever committed against its people? Without McCann Lumber there would be no community.

It was then that he saw her. He picked her face out of the crowd as if his gaze were drawn to it by a magnet, and the years fell away. He saw her as she'd been the first time he'd seen her, her sky-blue eyes twinkling with laughter, the sunlight gleaming on her bright red hair as she issued an impish challenge. *Poor Billy D., he can't get me. Can't get me. Can't get me.*

"Wanna bet?" he muttered, blinking in startled confusion when he realized he'd spoken aloud.

With his stomach churning, Bill glanced down at his speech, then crinkled the useless paper into a small wad. Decision made, he cleared his throat and spoke in a loud, clipped voice. "As of today, the McCann Lumber Company is back in business. I can't promise we'll go on full shifts until I've determined the scope of problems we're up against, but I can promise that there's going to be some big changes in the way this company operates. Those of you who were on the payroll before the shutdown can report back to work on Tuesday. We'll take things from there," he concluded tersely, unable to think of anything more to add.

Embarrassed by the rousing applause that greeted his niggardly speech, Bill stepped back from the lectern. After the sacrifice he'd just made, he deserved some sort of prize, but this town had only one thing he'd ever wanted and that was Gloria Hubbard. Now that Big Will was gone, nothing stood in the way of his having her and that knowledge eased some of the frustration he felt at being permanently tied down to a desk.

Rewarding himself with the pleasant thought of taking up with Glory again, Bill searched out her face in the crowd, but he surely didn't like what he saw once he found it. Her complexion was ashen, her bleak expression revealing to anyone who cared to look just how little she cared about his philanthropic decision. Everyone else in town might be applauding his willingness to stay, but Glory wanted him off the mountain permanently. Unable to resist the challenge, Bill shot her a brief, mocking grin before turning the floor back over to the mayor.

As Caleb shouted, ''Times are a-changin', folks, but some changes are for the best.'' Bill nodded in wry agreement, wishing he could see around the lectern, but then, he supposed, being an eyewitness to Glory's reaction when the mayor suggested that it was time to start celebrating his homecoming really wasn't necessary. Since as young children he'd been on the wrong end of her temper any number of times, he could easily picture the fiery sparks flashing in her big blue eyes.

Two

Glory followed along with the crowd on its way toward the dunking booth, hoping to camouflage herself amid the other numerous flowered sun dresses assembled on the town green. It had been almost a decade since she'd last seen Billy D. McCann, but he hadn't changed all that much physically, and unfortunately, her response to him hadn't changed that much, either. Indeed, her initial reaction to the sight of him had been much more violent than she'd ever anticipated and it had left her quaking in her five-and-dime sandals.

She'd forgotten just how good-looking he was, and how dark—dark hair, dark eyes, deeply tanned skin. For reasons she still couldn't fathom, she'd always been drawn to that darkness. A homebody herself, maybe she was attracted to the aura of adventure that hovered around his long, lean body like an unholy halo, but if not that, something in him had called out to something in her from the very first. Now the summons was more insistent than it had been when they'd been children, the feelings far stronger, even, than when they'd been teenagers.

At twenty-nine, Billy D. was no longer a teenager, but a mature man. To her dismay, Glory had to admit that the years had been kind to him. He was still as sexy as all get-out.

He was slightly taller now, and broader shouldered, yet his hips were still slender and those long, muscular legs of his could still make a pair of ordinary jeans look downright sinful. And she, Glory thought mournfully, for all her lack of voluptuous shape and imposing height, was a fully grown woman who'd wasted too many years trying her best to forget him.

Until today she thought she'd been successful, but when he'd gazed over the lectern straight into her eyes, the years had simply fallen away and she'd known that all of her efforts had been useless. He had flashed that vexing, white-toothed grin at her, just like he'd done a hundred times before, and her entire body had broken out in delicious shivers, exactly as it had when she'd been a moony adolescent. Only this time, Glory promised herself, she would rather die than admit that she had the slightest feeling for him. He'd rejected her once, cruelly and completely, but he would never get another chance—not if she could help it.

Billy D. had taught her many things in his time, but the harshest lesson of all had to do with female pride. With him, she'd never had any, and that had been her biggest mistake. The summer she'd turned sixteen, she'd even fooled herself into believing that she meant more to him than any other girl ever had, that he was falling in love with her, but then he'd shown her just how gullible she'd been.

Looking back on that tumultuous period of her life, Glory saw it as a miracle that he'd called a halt to their brief romance before her name could be added to the list of all his other female conquests. However, instead of being grateful for that blessing, she'd taken his rejection as proof of her total inadequacy in the seduction department. Gratefully, he'd left town shortly after that last humiliating rendezvous in Hunter's Grove, when she'd offered her pathetically immature body to him, so she hadn't been forced to watch him move on to much lusher and far-less-green pastures.

Just thinking about that horrible night made Glory's cheeks burn with shame, and according to the challenging smile he'd sent her way earlier, Billy D. McCann was still capable of being utterly hateful. Glory was just thankful that if nothing else, his surprising announcement today had negated any need for her to go asking for trouble. He and his son were staying in Hillsborough, just as her aunts, her brothers and apparently everyone else in town wanted—everyone, that was, but her.

"How are you, Glory? It's been a lot of years."

Not nearly as many as I'd like, Glory thought bitterly, wishing she were clinging to the arm of a tall, dark and handsome husband or at least a hunky, long-time boyfriend, as she forced herself to turn around and face the owner of that deep, distinctive voice.

"You haven't changed a bit," he observed.

Well, Glory decided fiercely, she would certainly prove him wrong on that score. Maybe she looked close to the same, but she'd added a fair degree of sophistication since the "good old days." While a coed, she'd dated several men who'd taken quite a liking to her less-than-voluptuous figure. The naive teenage girl he'd known no longer existed.

Unfortunately, up this close, Billy looked even better to her than he had at eighteen, and her mouth dried up as it always had around him. "Billy...eh... William...I mean Bill." She floundered nervously over his name and wanted to kick herself. Then, she saw his lips twitch, and she wanted to kick him instead.

"Bill's fine," he told her, cocking his head to one side as he looked her up one side and down the other. Those insolent dark eyes of his lingered for a moment on the bright pink ribbon tied around her loose top-knot, and he smiled fondly, as if remembering those warm summer nights when he'd gently pulled her ribbons away and watched in fascination as her long, red hair had tumbled down her back. He'd always seemed to like touching her hair, running his fingers through the shiny strands as if imagining—

Fists clenched at her sides, Glory dragged herself back to the present. "Bill," she repeated dutifully, then, hoping she sounded pleasant but emotionally detached, she admitted, "You haven't changed that much, either."

"It may not look like it, but I have," Bill said tightly, and Glory thought she heard not only a promise, but some kind of threat in his tone. But then, he'd always threatened her in one way or another, if not physically, then emotionally. As for his promises, well, there were names for unscrupulous types like him...unspeakably nasty names.

Disliking the vengeful trend of her thoughts, Glory decided that it would be wise if she stopped encouraging further conversation. Smiling dismissively, she turned around, once again facing the head of the line, but apparently Bill wasn't through trying to get under her skin. "I'd like you to meet my son, Jamie."

Glory closed her eyes as her heart contracted painfully, but by the time she turned back to acknowledge the introduction, her expression was once again serene. Knowing he'd had a child by another woman hurt her deeply, but that was the last thing she wanted him to know. Her deception didn't last long, however, for when she glanced down at the boy, she found herself staring into a pair of eyes as dark violet as nightshade—eyes the exact same shade as his father's.

"Jamie," she murmured, unable to stem the quaver in her voice as she noted the light sprinkle of freckles over his nose and the red cast to his unruly brown hair. "It's...very nice to meet you."

"You, too, ma'am," he replied graciously, but then a *clang* sounded from the dunking booth, and Mayor Bonner yelped just before the wood plank he was sitting on gave way. The crowd roared with laughter as Caleb went down in the water tank, and Jamie dashed forward for a better look.

Glory followed him with her eyes for a moment, then she turned back to Bill and lifted her chin. "He's a beautiful boy," she admitted honestly, biting her tongue to prevent herself from asking personal questions, especially the ones that were uppermost in her mind. *Did you run off and marry a woman with red hair and freckles, Billy D.? Did the resemblance between the two of us stop there?*

"Better not let him hear you say that," Bill warned with a chuckle. "At his age, he'd take that remark as an insult."

"Cute then," Glory revised.

Bill was inordinately pleased to discover that there were still some things in the world that didn't change. It appeared as if Gloria Hubbard still had the same giving nature that she'd had as a young girl. After the cruel way he'd once treated her, he hadn't expected a very warm reception, and the fact that she could find the generosity to compliment him on his son warmed a place in his heart that had remained bitterly cold for far too long.

With an engaging grin that had always achieved pleasant results with the fair sex, he questioned her choice of adjective, "Maybe you're thinking of handsome . . . like his father?"

As susceptible to that lopsided smile as the next woman, Glory found herself smiling back, but her enjoyment faded quickly as her thoughts returned to the boy's mother. "Ida May told us that your wife died in childbirth. I'm sorry. That must have been very hard on both you and Jamie."

Bill's jaw tightened. This wasn't the time or the place to get into lengthy explanations concerning Jamie's mother. On the other hand, accepting Glory's condolences for his loss made him feel like a hypocrite. "Jamie's mother and I were never married."

"Oh," Glory said, feeling like a fool. "I didn't know."

"You don't know a lot of things about me, Glory," Bill replied, unconsciously reverting to the less-formal version of her name. "But eventually, I'm afraid you and everyone else in this town are going to find out much more than you ever cared to."

Glory couldn't quite decide how to take that comment, especially since his tone had an almost... well...sinister edge. "You said before that I had hardly changed, well I'm not the same girl you left behind," she stated defensively, wondering if he'd changed as much over the years as she had, and if any of those changes were for the better. "For one thing, I've learned not to involve myself in matters that are none of my business."

Disliking the sudden remoteness in her tone, especially when he was feeling so warmly toward her, Bill smiled mockingly. "There was a time when everything I did was your business."

Well, that answered that question! Glory thought. He was still an insufferable, conceited so-and-so. "It used to be that I gave two hoots about you," she reminded him with saccharine sweetness. "But I was very young then, and very foolish."

"Very young and very beautiful," he corrected, using the low, caressing tone of voice that she'd never been able to forget. "And very desirable."

Bill stayed where he was only long enough to watch her mouth drop open before he edged through the crowd to locate his son, who had an exasperating tendency to get himself lost. He spotted Jamie clinging to the fence surrounding the dunking booth, and satisfied that the boy would stay put for another ten seconds, he turned around for one last look at Glory. She was still standing in the exact same spot as he'd left her, staring after him in bemusement.

Eyes sparkling with the kind of macho determination that he hadn't felt since a defiant teenage girl had made a fool of him in the town square, Bill sent her a silent message. *Chew on that for a while, Glory Hubbard, and see if you don't like the taste.*

The lumber mill had been closed down for over a month due to Big Will's fatal illness, but promptly at six o'clock Tuesday morning, just as Billy D. had promised, the whistle blew and work started again. For Glory this meant that she had to be prepared to take in at least twenty preschool children instead of the eight she'd had in her charge for the previous four weeks. Fortunately, when the children started arriving, so did the three young women who'd been assisting her at the day-care center before the mill had stopped running at full capacity.

"One of these days, Lorine Miller," Glory scolded the first woman to step through the open doorway of the large, one-story cement building, "you're going to have to get a phone up at your place."

"No need." Lorine tossed off that suggestion as forthrightly as she shooed loitering children into the playroom. As always, to Glory's continuing amazement, not one of the youngsters was intimidated by the woman who stood well over six feet tall and spoke to them in a gruff masculine-sounding voice. Like her, the children somehow sensed that Lorine was the gentlest of giants. "I knew you'd be wantin' me. So I came."

"I shouldn't have worried." Glory turned and held up a threatening finger as Cindy Potter and Becky Miller came through the door. In their early twenties, both women were married, and Becky was already the mother of five. "As for you two, I tried to reach you all weekend and there was never any answer."

"Ben and I were takin' advantage of the last days of our vacation," Cindy explained, a blissful smile on her thin, angular face. "It's probably the last one we'll ever get."

"I was up visitin' my ma up at the hollow," Becky said, pulling one hand away from her clinging four-year-old daughter and the other hand from her two-year-old son. "Go inside now, darlin's. I'll be right there," she directed with a gap-toothed smile before turning back to Glory. "My eldest brought the word that the mill was openin' up today, so I hightailed it back late last night. What with Tom out of work, I can't tell you how much we've been missin' my paycheck."

Betty Mae Turnbull, a middle-aged widow who was Glory's permanent assistant, was all smiles as she greeted the younger threesome. "Glory and I feared we'd be on our own all day with this posse of screamin' kids. Thank the good Lord you all came."

Glory agreed with that sentiment completely, and for more than the obvious reasons. Since opening the day-care center three years before, she'd become aware of several other services that she might offer to the community, and now she had three more fledgling concerns operating under her roof—a food co-op to reduce the price of groceries, a thrift shop for second-hand clothing and a folk-arts program to help local women increase, share and market their craft skills. Of course, most of the twenty or so women who worked for her were hired on a part-time basis, and her operations couldn't compare to McCann Lumber, but she could still be considered one of Hillsborough's leading employers.

Glory wondered what Bill McCann would say when he came across that information, then chided herself for thinking about him at all. As she'd told herself a zillion times since the picnic, she wanted no part of that man. So what did she care what he thought?

"Something wrong, Glory?" Becky asked.

Glory shook her head, forcing a certain somebody out of her brain. "Not since you three showed up," she replied, relief replacing her hostile expression. "Now I can help Marjorie and Kathy with the co-op this morning. We still have a ton of cheese to cut, ten hams to slice and twenty bushels of oranges to count before the other members start arriving."

"Best all of us get to it, then," Lorine said briskly, and scooped up a smiling toddler in her long, thin arms. "C'mon Riley Thomas, let's go find that pretty picture book and see if ol' Hooty Owl is still a bother to his furry friends."

Glory could hear the rest of the children clamoring to hear the story as she walked down the hall to the large room facing the main road into town. For the next two hours she helped to label and distribute food, then returned to the playroom to assist during snacktime. Before noon, she'd sent letters and made over twenty phone calls to local businesses seeking their donations for the next project on her list—a clinic that would provide decent health care for the poor. At lunchtime, she returned to the playroom to help dispense meals, supervised the children's outdoor play before nap time, and then, for the remainder of the afternoon and early evening, she helped her folk-arts center staff assign booths and organize events for the upcoming arts-and-crafts festival.

She always enjoyed her two-mile walk home, for it was one of the few times during the day when she could appreciate the majestic serenity of her mountainous surroundings.

Hillsborough might be located in one of the most economically depressed areas of the country, but to Glory, no place could ever be more abundant in beauty. In most sections, the land remained unspoiled, rich with forests and lush with summer vegetation, its lakes and rivers flowing with sparkling clean water.

As she walked along the winding dirt road at the base of McCann Mountain, Glory drew in a deep restorative breath. As always, the air was crispy cool and fragrant with the smell of wildflowers and pine and green grass. It was a little past dusk, so the sky wasn't filled with songbirds, but when she scanned the wild field adjoining the road, she counted two wild turkeys, four ruffed grouse and a huge swarm of wood warblers. She could hear the bullfrogs croaking when she jumped over Hickory Creek, and by the time she reached the tiny white-framed house nestled in the stand of spruce trees at the northern edge of the valley, the moon was coming up and the crickets were starting to sing.

As she sauntered up the stone walkway, she was humming, but she stopped abruptly when a dark shadow rose like a specter on her front porch.

"Who is that?" she asked nervously, but when there was no response other than the rhythmic creak of the recently vacated porch swing, she lost her fear. Obviously, scaring her to death was her eldest brother Kenny's latest idea for persuading her to see the folly in living alone. "Listen here, you mean-minded turkey! You can jump out at me from the bushes or drop down on me from a thousand trees and I still won't move back into town!"

As she marched up the porch steps, she demanded, "Now, how many more times am I going to have to tell you that before you and those other two mindless minions of yours get the message?"

"Once ought to do it," a man's voice replied, but it wasn't Kenny's voice, or David's or Zeke's. It was William Daniel McCann's!

"What are you doing here?" Glory gasped, coming to a complete halt on the top step as a broad set of shoulders encased in a navy-blue T-shirt, and a pair of long, lean legs wearing black jeans separated themselves from the deeper shadows on the porch.

With a familiarity that made her extremely nervous, Bill walked over to the front door and pounded his fist on a specific spot in the slat of painted wood nearest the light fixture. Immediately, the porch light came on, illuminating her pale white complexion and his sheepish face. "I didn't realize anyone was still living here," he admitted gruffly. "Ida May told me that after you kids grew up and left home, your aunts moved into a house in town."

"They did," Glory said, hoping he didn't notice the trembling in her legs as she forced herself to mount the last step. "But when I came back from college, they offered to rent it to me, and I took them up on the offer, much against the better judgment of my brothers. Those big, overprotective galoots don't think it's safe for me to live on my own, let alone in a place this far out from town."

"So I gathered," Bill replied, hiding a smile as he recalled her indignant tirade. "And I can understand where they're coming from. In this day and age, they've good reason to worry. It's not the same innocent world it was back when we were kids."

Glory recognized the voice of a world-weary cynic, but she was perceptive enough to also hear a certain wistfulness in his tone. "Is that what you're doing here?" she asked softly. "Looking for long-lost worlds?"

Bill had forgotten Glory's talent for reading his innermost thoughts and he didn't appreciate her insight any more now than he had when he'd been nine. "Maybe," he allowed grudgingly, then immediately changed the subject. "Kenny mentioned that your brother Jessie left town to make his own way in the world a year after I did. I always liked Jess. I suppose he's not much of a letter writer, but do you ever hear from him?"

Glory was no more eager than he was to get into some deep philosophical discussion, but neither was she that willing to discuss her absent brother. Having watched the two of them play together as boys, she'd willingly acknowledged that besides their ages, there'd been a number of other similarities between her best friend, Billy D., and her favorite brother, who'd grown into the black sheep of the Hubbard family. For that reason she heartily disliked admitting to any such comparisons.

In a tone as begrudging as the one he'd recently used, Glory acknowledged where Jessie Ray was, leaving out the part about him being a no-account drifter. "The last we heard, he'd just hired on at some big cattle ranch in Montana."

Unaware of her pique or the reason for it, Bill grinned and admitted, "I did that for a while myself before Jamie was born. It was good, honest work, but hard as hell on my poor butt."

Glory wished he hadn't referred to that particular portion of his anatomy. As a teenager, she'd been thoroughly fascinated by the sexy fit of his jeans, and it appalled her to discover that she still was. To make matters worse, when she forced her gaze back up to where it belonged, she discovered that Billy had observed her momentary lapse of discretion.

"Riding horses didn't ruin me," he informed her with an amused grin. "If that's what you were wondering."

A horrible liar, Glory still attempted to wiggle her way out of one of life's most embarrassing moments. "I—I thought I noticed a slight limp on the day of the picnic."

Glory should have remembered that the man was entirely too full of himself to allow her even the most harmless of fibs. "I noticed you noticing," he replied wickedly, taking what she saw as malicious delight in her bright red face.

Then, to her utter mortification, he reached out and chucked her indulgently under the chin. "A woman who can still blush. Speaking of innocence and lost worlds...."

Becoming more furious by the minute, Glory resisted the urge to stomp her foot and scream that she was no longer such a child. "You may like to think so," she managed in a disdainful tone, "but I'm not all that innocent anymore."

He cocked a disbelieving eyebrow. "Is that so?"

"In your estimation, this may be the back of beyond, but some of us are quite willing and able to move with the times."

"And you're one of those willing kind?"

Unaware of the dangerous intent behind the question, Glory asserted, "Most definitely!"

"Then being such a modern woman, this shouldn't come as any great shock to you," Bill said as he grasped her by the shoulders and pulled her into his arms.

The kiss was merely inquisitive to start with, but within a matter of seconds it changed into something far more ruthless and hungry. As soon as Bill got the delectable taste of her in his mouth, the craving of years overtook him and his tongue delved for more, savoring her sweetness, remembering those few precious times when he'd tasted her before.

He hadn't intended to kiss her just yet, but he usually gave a woman what she asked for, and as far as he was concerned, Glory had only herself to blame for this. Of course, she didn't realize that he'd been carrying a torch for her all these years, and she certainly couldn't have predicted how violently her claim of being experienced with men would provoke him. Bill was having a hard time explaining his reaction to himself, but now that he had her right where he wanted her, he intended to enjoy himself.

As for Glory, once back in his arms, she couldn't help herself. She accepted the intimate probing of his tongue without offering any protest, lost in the same euphoric daze of memories as he was. It had been so long since she'd been kissed by a man who made her feel like a desirable woman, a talent that Billy had possessed even as a teenager. Beneath the fragrant branches of the spruce trees in Hunter's Grove, he'd given her her first kiss, then taught her the true meaning of passion, and she'd never forgotten the lesson. Unfortunately, as her lips moved eagerly under his, she allowed herself to forget what had happened to her once her teacher had decided that lessontime was over.

Feeling the press of her soft breasts against his chest, Bill groaned and lifted his head before things got entirely out of hand. Breath ragged, he stared down at her swollen mouth. Glory stared dreamily back up at him, as if years hadn't passed since he'd last kissed her. "My, my, you *have* come a long way," Bill complimented, though there was more disappointment than flattery in his tone. "I guess you weren't lying about your discarded innocence, were you?"

The cynical twist to his lips brought Glory back to reality with a painful jolt. Seeing it, one part of her wanted to deny her previous claim, but another part was equally anxious to prove that she wasn't that pathetic innocent he'd left behind. "How could I be? I'm twenty-six years old."

"But never married," Bill said, his arms falling away from her shoulders as he leaned back against the door frame. Watching her face closely, he continued, "Or engaged, or even deeply involved with a man, if what Ida May tells me is true?"

Infuriated by the possibility that her meddling busybody of a cousin might have told him far more about her than he had any right to know, Glory offered what she hoped was a feasible explanation. "Have you forgotten? Anyone familiar with Ida May Potter only tells her what they want her to know. Otherwise, everyone else in town would be privy to their private business."

"No, I haven't forgotten," Bill replied, jaw clenching as he remembered the day his daddy had confronted him about his friendship with Glory. He'd always suspected that Ida May had been responsible for telling Big Will about the budding romance, but since their housekeeper had been much kinder to him than his own mother ever had, he'd never confronted the woman with his suspicion. Besides, after Big Will had gotten through with him that day, the damage had already been done, and as angry as he'd been with his daddy, he'd seen no purpose in blaming Ida May for revealing something he'd been gathering up the courage to tell the man himself.

If Glory hadn't tossed her head impatiently, capturing a beam of moonlight in her hair, Bill might have remained lost in those hated memories for several more seconds, but the provocative movement immediately reclaimed his full attention. "After tonight, another thing I won't forget is how well you kiss," he drawled, grinning at the indignant sparks that swiftly took fire in her beautiful eyes. "Or how much you seemed to enjoy mine. Since you've become such a modern woman, maybe when I come back we should make love and see how well we both enjoy that."

It took every ounce of fortitude Glory possessed but she managed not to react to his suggestive words like a morally outraged Victorian maiden. Lifting her chin, she took a step to his right, pointedly waiting for him to move aside so she could push open her storm door. When he did, she didn't jump through the door like a scalded cat, but took her time getting inside. Then, gazing calmly through the screen at him, she said, "I'd almost forgotten what an arrogant, conceited jerk you are. Now that you've reminded me, I live in hope that you'll *never* come back."

"But I am back, Glory," he reminded her, his smile gleaming in the moonlight. "And this time, I'm here to stay."

Glory grabbed the sturdy oak door she always left open in the summer and slammed it shut. Unfortunately, the wood wasn't thick enough to block out Bill's words of farewell or the jaunty whistle that followed after them. "Night darlin'. Sleep well and pleasant dreams."

As long as Billy D. McCann was living in Jessup County, Glory knew that she wouldn't feel safe closing her eyes, and her dreams would be far from pleasant. For the first time ever in her life, she slipped the heavy metal bolt through the matching groove and went to bed behind a locked door.

Three

——

Glory slept late the next Saturday morning, and since it was promising to be a very hot day, she opted to laze about outside on her porch rather than tackle any housework. A body had to relax sometime, and today, she decided, was her day. After pulling on a pair of cutoff denim shorts and an off-the-shoulder white blouse, she made herself a pitcher of lemonade, picked up the paperback mystery novel she'd been meaning to read and headed for her porch swing.

She was aware of movement in the forest surrounding her house long before the boy ducked out from beneath the branches of a spruce tree and spotted her sitting there. His first instinct was to run toward her, which told Glory he'd been wandering around lost for quite some time, but as soon as she waved at him, he straightened his narrow shoulders and slowed his pace.

Just like his daddy, this little guy was far too prideful, and he wasn't about to admit that he was either lost or afraid.

To hide the fact that he'd apparently been crying, he dashed a quick fist across his heat-flushed cheeks, then wiped his grubby hands on the backside of his jeans. Before venturing any closer to the porch steps, he jammed his hands into his pockets and attempted a jaunty whistle. In that moment he reminded Glory so much of Billy D. that her heart skipped a beat.

"Hi, lady, remember me?" he greeted as if he didn't have a care in the world, but by the number of scratches on his arms and the ragged tears in his blue T-shirt, Glory knew otherwise.

"I met you at the picnic," he reminded her, unable to camouflage his relief when she acknowledged the meeting with a nod. "You know my dad."

"That's right," Glory said, making no comment on his scruffy appearance or the slight quiver in his lower lip as she tried to put him more at ease. "I'm Glory Hubbard, an old . . . friend of your dad's and one of your closest neighbors."

The child brightened considerably as he walked across the porch with a macho swagger in his step. "Then you don't mind my comin' to visit uninvited," he concluded hopefully. "Ida May says folks around here expect other folks to be neighborly."

"That we do," Glory agreed, unable to help herself from grinning back at him as Jamie cast her a winning smile. She tried not to be affected by the unruly shock of brown hair that fell over his forehead or the nonchalant stance that came so naturally to him, but this boy was definitely his father's son, and Glory was drawn to him despite herself. "You're welcome to come see me anytime."

Someone had taught the youngster to respect his elders, for he bestowed a proper title on her as he replied, "Thank you, Miz Hubbard."

Though he wasn't that long past the cradle, it was obvious that Jamie McCann wouldn't accept being treated like a baby, and Glory couldn't bring herself to hurt his burgeoning masculine dignity. If he wanted to pretend that this was purely a social call, she was happy to oblige him. Having been lost in the woods many times herself, she knew what it felt like to be told how foolish she'd been. Even at Jamie's age, she'd been smart enough to figure that out for herself.

"I've known your dad since he was a boy almost as little as you," she remarked conversationally.

"Really?"

"Really," Glory said, understanding the child's doubt that his big strong daddy had ever been that small. After the run-in she'd had with the big man a few days earlier, she was having some trouble remembering that fact herself and a great deal of difficulty forgetting a few other things about him, like how wonderful his warm lips had felt plundering hers. "You look a lot like him."

"'Cept for my freckles." Jamie sighed, his disgusted expression making it obvious that he'd already experienced some ridicule over the tiny bright spots on his face.

Cursed with four blond brothers who didn't have a freckle between them, Glory knew all about that kind of teasing. Pointing to the slight gold dusting across her own nose, Glory declared, "I happen to like freckles. Some of the very best people I know have them.''

Jamie studied her face for a few seconds, then puffed out his chest. ''I like 'em, too,'' he said, and they shared an understanding grin.

Gesturing for the child to join her on the porch swing, Glory brought out glasses and poured them each some lemonade. She knew from experience that boys his age usually had more energy than they knew what to do with, but this little one was supremely grateful to be asked to sit down, and he hurried to comply with her request. ''Out exploring, were you, Jamie, before you dropped in for a neighborly visit?''

''Yes, ma'am,'' he admitted, brushing the mud off the seat of his pants before he settled himself on the swing. Once again, Glory was impressed by his good manners until he accepted the glass she offered him with both hands and slurped it all down before she had taken one sip of hers. ''Me and my dad like to explore places, but he was . . . eh . . . too busy to come with me today.''

''I see. Well, you've walked an awful long way from your house this morning. Maybe two or three miles,'' Glory observed, trying not to smile as his dark eyes settled eagerly on the lemonade pitcher. ''You must be pretty tired and thirsty after travelling that far. Care for another glass?''

''Yes, please,'' he replied politely, and proceeded to gulp down her second offering as noisily as he had the first. After wiping his mouth with the back of his hand, he took a deep breath and admitted, ''I don't know my way around here too good yet. Do you know a faster way for me to get back home?''

"A faster way?"

Reluctantly he conceded, "My dad gets kind of worried when I'm gone too long."

Knowing the man's volatile temperament, Glory bet that was an understatement, but her expression remained matter-of-fact as she pointed to the road. "If you knew how to drive a car, that way would be faster, but walking up the road will take you another hour or so."

Jamie's shoulders slumped dejectedly. "That long?"

"I'm afraid so," Glory replied gently. "Maybe I should call your dad and have him come pick you up."

Pride flew out the window when she made that suggestion. The child's flushed face paled to the color of chalk and his dark eyes welled up with tears. "He's going to do it to me this time for sure."

Concerned by his violent reaction, Glory prompted, "Do what?"

Lower lip turned down ruefully, Jamie cried, "Dad says I'm harder to keep track of than a mangy coon dog, and if I don't stay where I'm s'posed to, he's going to put me on a leash."

"I don't think he meant that literally, Jamie," Glory assured, then seeing that the child didn't understand her meaning, she explained, "He just meant that he'll have to keep a closer eye on you in the future."

"Uh-uh," the boy insisted miserably. "When I was little, he put me on a leash lots of times."

Glory was horrified. She didn't want to believe that the man might be capable of such cruelty toward a mere baby, especially when he himself had suffered so much at the hands of overstrict parents, but a child as young as Jamie wouldn't think to lie about something so awful. On the other hand, when it came to describing corporal punishment, young boys had been known to exaggerate. "Your father didn't actually put you on a dog's leash, did he?" she forced herself to ask, but with one glance into a pair of soulful dark eyes, she had her answer and Glory felt a sick sensation in the pit of her stomach.

Jamie nodded his head solemnly, obviously sensing a sympathetic soul and a possible ally when the time came to face his irate parent. The last time he'd gotten himself lost like this, he'd been gone for a whole day. Once the policeman had dropped him off at home, he'd gotten the spanking his father had threatened to give him a number of times before, and he sure didn't want another one. "Yes, ma'am, and I didn't like it at all, or getting hit, neither," he complained, thrusting out his lower lip as he gazed beseechingly up at her. "But when I'm very bad, my dad don't care what I like."

"Well, I care, and nothing you've done today makes you bad! You may have done a wrong thing, but that doesn't make you a bad person."

Protective instincts fully aroused, Glory took one of Jamie's hands in her own and gave the small palm a soothing pat, but her voice rose higher and higher with every word she uttered. "And I'll tell you another thing, young man. I'm not afraid of Billy D. McCann, and no matter how high and mighty he thinks he is, he's going to hear exactly how I feel about hitting a child or putting him on a leash!"

Wide-eyed, Jamie stared at her. "You're gonna yell at my dad!"

"It won't be the first time," Glory admitted darkly as she grabbed Jamie's hand and drew him off the swing.

"But, lady, he's way bigger than you," Jamie said, an awed expression on his face as he trotted along obediently beside her into the house.

"'The bigger they are, the harder they fall,'" Glory quoted fiercely.

Jamie winced, and Glory assumed it was due to some misplaced sense of filial loyalty, until she felt a small tug and realized that she was squeezing his hand much too hard. "Sorry, sweetie," she apologized. "Now let's put some medicine on those scratches of yours before they start to fester."

They were halfway to the bathroom before Jamie seemed to remember the last time someone had tended to similar injuries, and he immediately pulled back on his hand. "I don't want no medicine on 'em. Medicine hurts like anything!"

"Not my kind," Glory promised, and oddly enough, the child allowed himself to be ushered into her bathroom.

"Okay," he agreed, sitting down on the edge of the bathtub. "But if it does, I'm tellin' my dad."

Glory smiled at that warning, glad to hear that the boy still looked upon his father as his protector. Maybe her childhood nemesis wasn't as lousy a parent as she thought. Still, any man who would treat his precious son like a dog deserved a good talking to, and she was just the person to do it.

"Hey! That didn't hurt at all," Jamie announced in surprise once the last scratch was swabbed down with the soothing white paste. "That's pretty neat stuff."

"That stuff is the Hubbard family remedy for all that ails ya'," Glory informed him, then wrinkled her nose. "But take my word for it, sweetie, it's much nicer to wear than to swallow."

Jamie took a sniff of his arm and grinned up at her, then his brow furrowed and he asked curiously, "Why do you keep calling me 'sweetie'?"

Glory wasn't certain if he was offended or not, so she said with a shrug, "I think you're a very sweet boy, but if you'd rather I didn't call you that, I won't."

Jamie looked into her eyes, his gaze half wondering, half wary, and Glory felt a bittersweet flutter in her heart. She remembered a long-ago summer day and another pair of dark eyes conveying the same expression, another young boy calling out to her to fill a lonely void inside himself with her laughter and love, but wary of her motives for wanting to give so much of herself to a person she didn't even know. She remembered her own vehemence as she'd exclaimed, *I can care about you iffen I want to,* and she had to fight those same feelings again. It was obvious to her that this poor child was desperately lonely and as starved for affection as his father had been the first time she'd met him.

After a long considering pause, Jamie's lips curved upward in a sheepish smile, and he didn't look at her as he murmured, "I like it a lot."

Resisting the strong urge to hug him, Glory turned on the faucets in the sink and washed the medicine off her fingers. "C'mon, then sweetie," she declared evenly, once she'd wiped her hands dry. "I'll call your dad and you and I can eat some lunch while we wait for him to come."

They didn't have very long to wait, but Jamie wasn't awake when a beat-up pickup truck came racing down the road and screeched to a stop in front of her house. He'd fallen asleep over his peanut butter sandwich and Glory had picked him up and carried him into her bedroom, making sure to close the door behind her. After his fearful ordeal in the woods, the child was completely exhausted. He needed his sleep, and in Glory's opinion, he didn't need to be within earshot when she exchanged a few well-chosen words with his daddy.

With that goal firmly in mind, she took up guard on the porch, crossing her arms over her chest defensively as Bill strode purposefully up her walkway. If the son looked scruffy, the father looked like he'd been pulled backward through a hollow swamp log. His black hair was slick with sweat, his handsome face was smudged with mud and his skin mottled. His shirt was ripped open at the shoulder, exposing a deep gash, and his boots and blue jeans were coated with the kind of green slime that could always be found surrounding the peat bog.

"Where is he?" he demanded loudly, stepping past Glory as if she weren't even there. "I've been searching for that wayward little devil for the past four hours!"

The man was practically double her size, but when she was two-fisted angry, Glory was willing to take on a giant, and before this one gained entry into her house she slipped in front of him to bar the door. "Jamie's sleeping," she informed him tartly. "And you're not going to touch that poor baby until I say so!"

Poor baby? Cocking one eyebrow, Bill looked down at her, startled by the fiery light of condemnation in her eyes as much as her intent to keep him away from his son. With only another second's consideration, he'd figured out what was going on. Jamie had recognized a bleeding heart when he saw one, and hoping to avoid a well-deserved punishment, he'd done a fine job of playing on Glory's compassionate heartstrings.

For a six-year-old, Jamie was highly resourceful and Bill couldn't wait to hear which one of his many methods he'd used to persuade Glory over to his side. "I'm not?"

"No, you're not!" Glory exclaimed, poking one finger into his chest for emphasis as she continued her speech. "I don't care if he did run off without telling you and got lost. That sweet, inquisitive child has already suffered enough and he's absolutely scared to death of what you're going to do to him."

Unaware that Glory was under the impression that he wasn't above the use of cruel and unusual punishment, Bill growled, "After what he's put me through this morning, that sweet child had *better* be scared. Damned good and scared!"

When he reached over her shoulder to push open the door, Glory read an intent in his smouldering dark eyes that horrified her. Pulling herself up to her full five feet two inches, she plastered herself against the white metal screen. "You can't mean to hit him!"

"Oh, I won't hit him, but he'll never take off on me again," Bill replied tightly, on the point of losing his already taxed patience. What he did or didn't do with his son was no one's business but his own, and if

Gloria Eloise Hubbard didn't move out of his way fairly soon, she was going to learn that pertinent lesson right along with Jamie.

"Now step aside, Glory," he ordered. "Protecting him like this isn't going to help him. It's just making me madder. I warned him what would happen if he went beyond the yard, but he chose to disobey me, and he's going to be punished for it whether you like it or not!"

"Punished how?" Glory cried out in desperation, very much aware that she was no match for him if he chose to reach down and set her aside. "Like you were punished by *your* daddy? Are you going to take a switch to him, Billy D.? Will it make you feel better to draw a little blood? Isn't that what it always took before Big Will stopped whippin' you?"

Silence greeted that question—a killing silence. Glory stood motionless, afraid to move as she watched fury coil through Bill's body like a living thing, stiffening his spine, clenching his hands into fists, clamping his teeth together as a pulse jerked to life in his jaw.

"Is that what you think?" he asked as the blood drained from his face then surged back again in an angry tide.

Glory cringed away from him, shocked by his physical response to her admittedly cruel but very necessary questions. Unfortunately, the door was still behind her and there was no space to run. When he opened his mouth to speak again, she turned her face to the side as if expecting him to strike her, a reaction that only heightened the agonizing tension snaking between them.

"Is that what you think?" he repeated, in a tone all the more heartrending because of the desolation it contained. "Knowing what kind of punishment I took as a kid, do you actually think I would do the same to my son?"

Meeting his eyes, Glory didn't think so, not anymore, but it was too late to sheath her claws. She'd already cut into a place she knew to be his most vulnerable. Seeing his hurt, she was desperate to make amends but unable to do so without making matters worse for Jamie. "I didn't want to think so," she explained desperately. "I still don't want to...."

"But?"

Glory closed her eyes, too ashamed to look at him.

"Glory," Bill persisted in a scathing tone.

Reluctantly, she told him how she'd arrived at her erroneous conclusion. "Jamie said that you hit him when he was bad and...that—that you leashed him up like a dog. What else was I to think?"

Her plaintive question was an answer in itself. Bill ordered himself to take deep regular breaths to slow down his heartbeat and cool off his blood. He knew damned well that for Glory, when confronted with a frightened child, there was no other way for her to think. As long as he'd known her, with or without having any real proof of their supposedly weakened condition, she'd always placed herself firmly on the side of those she perceived to be defenseless or hurt. And, when challenged, she would fight tooth and nail to protect the downtrodden.

Bill also knew that his little boy was capable of making a grown man cry just by tearing up himself. If he himself could be suckered by a pair of brimming brown eyes and a quivering lower lip, Glory hadn't stood a chance. "If you'd ever gotten beyond Jessup County," he began, "you'd be familiar with a dandy new invention. It's very effective in large crowds where it's hard to keep track of little people, especially kids like Jamie, who are so easily distracted. It consists of a three-foot-long plastic coil and two wide Velcro strips, one to go around his wrist and one for mine."

"Oh, dear," Glory whispered, beginning to feel as backward as he obviously thought she was.

Bill nodded. "If you'd ever lost a three-year-old in a football stadium or watched him dash off a bus at the wrong stop, you'd have the same kind of appreciation for the Kiddie Kord as I do."

Glory sighed, feeling worse by the second.

"As for hitting," Bill continued relentlessly, "when the young man in question ducked under a coat rack and vanished inside one of the biggest shopping malls in Texas, he felt the flat of my hand on the seat of his jeans about two minutes after the local police brought him home. Which, I might add, was accomplished within eight hours of his disappearance, since I'd enlisted the aid of every law enforcement agency in the country to locate the whereabouts of my poor, innocent baby boy and the perverted fiend I was sure had abducted him."

Glory swallowed hard as she asked the next logical question. "I take it that no kidnapping occurred?"

"You take it right," Bill said tersely, unable to recall that particular incident without feeling his stomach roll. "While I was giving his description to the cops, Jamie was having the time of his life in the petting zoo exhibit. After I tanned his behind, he even had the nerve to ask me if we could go back to the mall and buy him a puppy.''

"He didn't!''

"Oh, yes, he did. According to him, he was only trying to do me a favor.''

"A favor?''

"You see, the puppies were on sale.''

To keep the bubble of laughter from escaping her lips, Glory covered her mouth with her hand. If she'd found herself in a similar situation, she wouldn't consider it a laughing matter, but since it was Bill who had to contend with the problem, it struck her as highly amusing. Apparently itchy feet was a genetic trait, as was pure unmitigated gall. Of course, she'd never approved of the way Big Will and Lorraine McCann had disciplined their irrepressibly wayward son, but she did have some sympathy for their frustration in dealing with him.

"Don't say it,'' Bill warned, reading her mind. "No matter what stunts I pulled as a kid, I don't deserve the kind of suffering Jamie puts me through.''

Glory wasn't too sure of that, but she thought it prudent not to say so. "It *does* sound as if he's led you a merry chase a time or two.''

"Or three or four,'' Bill corrected sardonically. "And I should have come down on him a lot harder the first time, but he has me wrapped around his little finger and he knows it.''

Since she looked on Bill as a man who didn't need anyone, Glory was astonished by his confession, and he surprised her even more by admitting, "The kid's all I've got and I love him.''

"I'm so sorry for misjudging you," Glory murmured softly. "But if you remember what a sucker I am for a good sob story, perhaps you'll understand. It's just that Jamie is so...so..."

"Fragile-looking beneath all his cute macho posturing," Bill finished for her. "You don't have to tell me. Believe me, I know."

Lips twitching, Glory pushed open the screen door and led the way into her house. "He's fairly small for his age. Was he born prematurely?" she asked curiously, hoping Billy wouldn't remind her of her claim that she no longer asked about things that were none of her business.

He didn't, but his dark eyes became a full shade darker as he said, "By almost three months. For a while there, I didn't know if he was going to make it."

Glory sensed there was far more to the story than what Bill was telling her, but his closed expression made her think better about prying further. "He's in here," she informed him as she opened the door to her bedroom. "And he's still sound asleep."

Unaware that the man behind her had developed a sudden interest in what she was wearing instead of what she was saying, Glory gazed affectionately at the small boy cuddled up on her bed. "Naughty or not, he'd put in an awfully tough morning. Couldn't we postpone waking him for just a little while yet?"

"Sure," Bill agreed at once, glancing over at the double bed and wishing that he and his son could trade places. Although Glory was still small, she'd definitely filled out in all the right areas, and knowing what she felt like in his arms, he was having a devil of a time keeping his hands off her. Enviously, he saw that Jamie's face was nestled against a floral-covered pillow, and he could easily picture Glory's head resting there with his resting beside it. Of course, neither one of them would be sleeping.

"Tell you what," he suggested. "I'll run home and get cleaned up, then come back to retrieve him."

As they both backed silently out of the room, Glory glanced at the sad state of his clothes. "Great idea."

Bill chuckled. "That offensive, am I?"

Oblivious to the fact that she'd taken his hand as she led the way to her front door, Glory said, "Remember that time you and I went froggin' in Miller's Swamp and you climbed up on that dead ol' oak tree? I'd say you look and smell about the same today as you did back then."

"You could have warned me that I was doing my high-wire act over a stink hole," Bill complained, loving the feel of her warm fingers clasped in his and amazed at the intensity of feeling her platonic touch aroused in him. "And you didn't have to laugh so blamed hard when I fell in."

Wearing the pious I-told-you-so expression that had always exasperated him as a boy, Glory sniffed, "A show-off deserves to be laughed at."

They'd reached the front door, but before Bill walked outside, he succumbed to the mischievous urge he hadn't had in years. "And the self-righteous deserve to be humbled."

Glory squeaked in surprise as Bill jerked on her hand and she stumbled against his side. In a mock attempt to be helpful, he brought both arms around her, making sure that her pristine white blouse absorbed a bit of mud and the telling fragrance of bog slime before she was allowed to right herself. Instead of losing her temper, she giggled and gave him a harmless punch in the stomach.

"It's a purely sad man who takes his own failings out on others, Billy D. McCann," she scolded, falling into the lilting speech of their youth as if no time had passed since those days when they'd been childhood playmates. "And you've got to be the saddest body I ever did know in my life."

As he gazed down into her laughing blue eyes, Bill's chest swelled with an overwhelming surge of sentimentality. He wasn't used to teasing or being teased any more now than he had been as a boy, but now as then, he willingly followed her lead. "Being so perfect and all, I suppose you think you can fix what ails me, don't you, Li'l Bit?"

Glory refused to read anything more into that challenging question than she would've when she'd been seven. Waggling a finger at him, she admonished, "I don't know iffen that's possible, Billy D. What you just done makes you a right poorly person."

Swallowing the sudden ache in his throat, Bill gave her a playful slap on the behind before pushing his way out the door. He didn't dare turn back and look at her for fear she would be able to tell what he was thinking. *Couldn't you at least give it a try, Glory Hubbard? For you can't rightly imagine just how poorly and sad I've been all these years away from you.*

Four

——

Jamie was still asleep when Bill came back to fetch him, which was just fine with Bill. When Glory suggested that they spend the time waiting on the well-shaded front porch, Bill prayed that his son would sleep the entire afternoon away. After the horrendous week he'd just put in at the office, sharing a glass of freshly squeezed lemonade and a porch swing with a lovely young woman dressed like Daisy Mae was his idea of paradise, especially when that woman happened to be Gloria Hubbard.

Wishing that he'd chosen to change into something cooler than a clean pair of jeans and a double-knit shirt, Bill leaned back on the wood-slat seat, luxuriating in a variety of pleasant sensations all at once. Over the past few days, he'd been struck a number of times by the surprising knowledge that he'd missed this backwoods section of the country. Considering how he'd felt when he'd left, he'd never thought he would experience any kind of nostalgia over this place, but it actually felt kind of good to be back.

With each rhythmic motion of the swing, he was greeted with the wonderful sights, sounds and smells he'd simply taken for granted as a youth. Although the porch beams obstructed some of his view, he could look up and see the craggy boulders and magnificent virgin spruce that formed a mysterious natural circle atop McCann Mountain. Ignoring the gray stone of the chimney he could see through the trees, he focused instead on the waterfalls that sprung forth from a crack in the south slope. That cascade of white water had always fascinated him, as had the dancing rainbows of mist that hung over the shadowy forest below it.

When he lifted his face, a cool mountain breeze rustled his hair and favored his nose with the delicate fragrance of heather, white pine and rosebay rhododendron. From the open field behind the house, he could hear the joyful chorus of summer songbirds, and high up in the surrounding trees, the cicadas were complaining about the unusually hot and humid weather.

When he thought back, Bill could remember other days just like this one—long, lazy summer days when the sun had beat down hotly on his bare head and tanned his skin to a deep mahogany brown. Then, as now, the porch swing he and Glory had shared had squeaked on each backward push and the gallons of lemonade they'd shared had been ice cold and tart. The old Hubbard aunts had made the best lemonade he'd ever tasted, and they must have passed down the recipe to their niece, for he couldn't detect a difference. As always, it tasted marvelous on the way down, but he gained even more enjoyment from watching the woman beside him sipping hers.

In many ways she was still the same Glory, but the years had wrought some captivating changes in her. There was no doubt about it. His L'il Bit was definitely "all growed" now, and astoundingly sexy in places he'd never even thought to check before.

For one thing, she'd developed a very delectable fullness to her lower lip, and when her tongue came out to lick the sugary corners of her mouth, Bill had to clench his teeth to keep himself from offering to complete the task himself. It had also come to his notice, while he'd followed her out to the porch and she'd bent over to pour his lemonade, that for all her lack of height, she had an extremely shapely pair of legs, a tight, sweet bottom and such slender hips that her denim shorts had the provocative tendency to expose her navel every time she inhaled.

As for her breasts, she still couldn't brag that much about size, but in Bill's opinion, what was there was Daisy Mae perfect. He also knew that no matter how "modern" she now claimed to be, she would be horrified to learn that her pink-and-white polka-dot halter clearly outlined her exquisite shape, right down to her pert nipples, or that a man's gaze couldn't help but be attracted to them and the smooth expanse of peach-toned skin exposed between her navel and breasts. Bill, however, was uncomfortably aware of her near nakedness as he guzzled down the remainder of his lemonade and leaned over the side of the swing to place the empty glass down on the sagging porch floor.

Since he also knew that she wouldn't appreciate his prurient interest, he allowed himself only a sweeping gaze down the length of her beautifully tanned legs. Once he'd progressed down as far as her pretty pink toes, he should have given up on his visual occupation, but he couldn't resist treating himself to one last lingering glance at the rest of her body as he set the swing back into motion with his foot. He rested his eyes for a long pleasurable moment on her breasts, but finally managed to switch his focus up to her face, only to discover that the supreme effort of will it had taken him to reach that point had all been for naught.

Glory's cheeks were the color of ruby-red roses, her eyes wide and wary. Immediately, Bill knew that he'd been caught staring and that Glory was in no doubt as to what he'd been staring at. She also clearly understood exactly what he'd like to do with everything he saw, and her reaction to the knowledge told him that if she wasn't still a virgin, she was the next closest thing to one.

Ridiculously pleased by this proof that her sexual experience was grossly exaggerated, he glanced sideways at her blushing face and warned, "One of these days, you're going to change your mind about wanting me to make love with you, and the moment you do, I'm going to take you up on that offer you once made me."

Glory wanted to argue. She wanted to fuss and fume at him the way she used to when they'd been children. She especially wanted to punish him for reminding her of the most embarrassing moment in her life, but no scathing retort came to mind. His intensely personal and extremely thorough survey of her body had so obliterated her defenses that all she could manage was a humiliatingly breathless, "Is that so?"

"Mmm-hmm, and we're both going to enjoy it more now than we would have when we were a pair of kids," Bill promised huskily, removing the empty lemonade glass from her fingers and placing it beside his. As he captured her trembling hand and pressed it down on her own bare thigh, her eyes widened. "Much more."

Smiling at her shocked expression, he brushed his knuckles over her warm skin. Anticipating her instinctive need to clamp her legs together, he trailed one finger up and down her clenched thigh muscles, gratified by her sharp intake of breath. "In fact, I'm going to make it so damned good for you that you'll want to repeat the offer over and over again instead of taking it back like you did the last time."

Billy D. McCann had always known how to get to her, but he'd never employed the kind of under-handed tactics he'd begun using the other night and was continuing today. As much as she would like it to be otherwise, Glory was forced to admit that she was no match for him in this area. If memories of that hungry kiss he'd stolen weren't enough torment, the erotic stroke of his fingers on the sensitive insides of her clenched thighs was making her whole body tingle, and she liked the feeling too much to rise to the verbal challenge he issued along with this ruthlessly sensual onslaught. At the moment she didn't feel up to taking back anything she might ever have said to him, too absorbed in the agonizing thrill of his touch to formulate a single coherent thought.

As he watched her lips part with the need for more oxygen, Bill smiled to himself. Glory's feelings had always been as easy to see as the freckles on her face, and at that moment, her pleasure was greater than her mistrust. Taking advantage of her vulnerable condition, he leaned over to nuzzle the tender skin at her nape, lifting her hair away to nibble at her with his teeth. Encouraged by her lack of protest, he took gentle possession of her ear lobe with his mouth, and her rapid breathing told him exactly how much she liked the feel of his lips on her.

At least he could still count on her physical reactions to his lovemaking. Even the time when she'd thought he was kissing her as punishment for pushing him into the municipal fountain, her pleasure had been obvious. She'd trembled wildly in his arms, just as she was trembling now.

"Let me have your mouth, Glory," he whispered, and she obediently turned her face up to his.

Bill felt her soft lips moving under his with a sense of wonder—wonder because he now realized that her eagerness didn't come from experience. She was responding like this because *he* was the one kissing her. The other night she'd been too caught off guard to protest, and he'd jumped to some very erroneous conclusions. Today, when he slid his tongue into her mouth he could tell by her tiny shocked gasp that she still didn't know a great deal about this kind of kissing.

What she lacked in finesse, however, she certainly made up for in enthusiasm. As chauvinistic as that made him, Bill was glad she hadn't honed her sexual skills on other men while he'd been away. Now that he was back in town for good, he wanted to be the one to teach her all there was to know about kissing and every other intimacy that could be shared between a man and a woman—starting now!

Somewhere in the back of her mind, Glory knew that she shouldn't be letting Bill caress her like this, yet she couldn't find the will to stop either him or herself. All the long years of loving him, missing him, dreaming about him, came together in a burst of need that made her heart run wild. As her eager mouth answered his, she slid her fingers into his thick black hair, satisfying herself with the silky texture she'd yearned so desperately to feel again. And, with each breath she drew, she refreshed her depleted sources with the masculine smell she craved—the intoxicating, dangerous, mysterious smell of Billy D. McCann.

She might have gone on kissing him, touching him, revelling in the pleasure of being with him again, if he'd restricted his attentions to her mouth, but Bill shocked her back to instant awareness by shifting her halter aside and cupping her bare breast in his large, warm palm. Before she was able to gather her scattered wits together, he was taking much greater liberties than he'd ever tried in the past. With a smooth, expert motion, both of her breasts were uncovered and her nipples captured between his caressing fingers.

As he tenderly rolled the sensitive peaks into throbbing nubs, all Glory could manage was a helpless plea. "Please, Billy...please don't do this to me!"

Bill's breathing was as ragged as hers, but he immediately drew his hands away. He couldn't, however, command his eyes to behave as easily. He looked down at her with blatant possession in his gaze, and Glory's breath caught in her throat as her nipples tightened even more beneath his intent scrutiny. Embarrassed, she lifted her arms to cover herself, but he held her wrists, stopping her. "Your breasts are beautiful, Glory, small, but perfect."

"Oh, please!"

"And so responsive. All I have to do is look at them and your nipples contract like pretty pink rosebuds. I like that."

"Billy!"

With an indulgent sigh, Bill pulled her halter up and retied the strings around her neck. "You shouldn't be embarrassed, you know. You're capable of doing the same thing to me," he informed her kindly, hoping to vanquish the fiery blush beating in her cheeks. "You always were, even if you weren't aware of it."

Glory shook her head in furious denial, frightened by the realization that she might very well be fighting a lost cause. "I don't want to do the same to you," she lied frantically. "Not now or ever."

"You can tell yourself that if you want to, but your body says something else entirely," Bill replied arrogantly.

"I don't care what my body says," Glory insisted in desperation, then blurted out the reason she felt that way. "You hurt me very badly once, and I won't be hurt by you again, William McCann."

Bill's fingers went still on her leg, but instead of removing his hand, he covered her palm and gently squeezed. "I know," he admitted gruffly. "But at the time, I didn't have very much of a choice."

Glory glared at him. "At the time, your precious freedom meant more to you than I did. I loved you, but you didn't like having those kind of strings attached, did you? Even as a boy, all you ever talked about was getting away. The instant you felt I was getting too close, that I might expect you to stay, you cut me out of your life in the cruelest way possible. You didn't have the courage to tell me the truth, so you did your best to make me believe that I was inadequate."

Bill had spent years wondering what kind of conclusions she'd drawn from his questionable actions that summer. Now that he did know, he felt the same helpless frustration that he'd felt when he was eighteen. Gazing up at the gray stone chimney that flawed the natural beauty of McCann Mountain, he swore silently. *May you rot in hell, you unfeeling bastard.* Despite his desire to erase the past, male pride kept him from defending himself to Glory. "So that's what you think."

"That's what I know."

Glory had always known why he'd run off, but knowing why and accepting it were two entirely different matters, especially when his decision had caused her and so many others such unbearable heartache. In her opinion, Billy's desire to be free of the constraints placed upon him by his wealthy family had been a selfish one, as was his total rejection of his father. Being a member of any family, even a difficult one like his, meant that a person had certain responsibilities, and a mature person learned how to handle them. In her book, running away from his problems with Big Will instead of confronting them had been a childish solution, and his decision to leave town had resulted in some very far-reaching consequences, not excluding her own broken heart.

Big Will might have been a strict, overbearing father with unrealistic expectations when it came to his son, but after his wife had died, the only one left for him to care about had been Billy. The man may not have shown it often enough, but Glory was sure that in his own way, he'd loved his son. Regrettably, he'd placed all of his hopes and dreams for the future of the company on Billy's shoulders at a very young age, never taking time to realize that his son hadn't shared those dreams.

When Billy had deserted him within a year of his wife's death, Big Will had simply stopped caring about anything at all but the oblivion he could find inside a whiskey bottle. According to her oldest brother, Kenny, there had been occasions when Big Will hadn't shown up at the office for weeks at a time. Under the guidance of such an apathetic owner, McCann Lumber had suffered, and as the company went, so had gone its employees.

To make up for declining profits, wages had been cut. Some employees had their hours reduced, while others had theirs lengthened. Kenny had been lucky to keep his office job, but the younger boys, David and Zeke, hadn't been so fortunate. Along with the majority of other loggers, they'd been laid off early on in the slow down. Zeke had eventually found a part-time job with a plywood company over in the next county, but David was still waiting to be called back to work. Other local men, full-timers who'd had their hours cut in half, had been forced to take on two or more other jobs just to make ends meet.

Being such a small, closely knit community, one man's hardship was felt by all. When the man who happened to own half the town fell on hard times, it meant a near calamity for everyone else. As the support of McCann Lumber steadily declined, folks had to search for assistance farther and farther afield. Some people had relocated. Others now drove long distances to work every day, and within the past year, Glory knew of at least seven local families who'd had no other choice but to apply for welfare.

Of course, Glory realized, it wouldn't be fair to blame Bill for all the varied ills of the community. And, to his credit, he'd finally agreed to step in before the lumberyards and paper mill had been closed down permanently, but that didn't mean that there weren't going to be many dark days still ahead. If it was possible to bring company operations back to what they'd once been, it was going to take hard work and plenty of time.

Knowing how close the company had been to going out of business, Glory couldn't help but think that everyone, including herself, would've been better off if Bill had never left town in the first place. Friends, relatives, neighbors—people she dearly loved—had paid a high price for his selfish teenage rebellion. If it were too late for McCann Lumber to be saved, many of them would keep right on paying. And why should any of them trust that Bill wouldn't take off again when the going got rough?

Watching the fleet of ambivalent expressions that passed over her features, Bill sighed in resignation.

Glory might enjoy his kisses. She night even surrender herself willingly to his brand of lovemaking, but
sexual attraction was only one of many feelings she
had for him. According to the antagonistic look on her
face, getting back into her good graces was going to be
as big a challenge as making the company profitable
again.

"Didn't your aunts ever tell you that it's dangerous
to scowl like that?" he asked, forcing a grin. "Keep it
up and your face just might stay that way."

Having heard that warning numerous times during
her childhood, Glory felt the beginnings of a smile
tugging at the corners of her mouth, but before she
gave into that urging, she switched the subject.
"Kenny tells me that you've got a mind to make some
innovative changes in company operations."

"I've been working on a few new ideas, yes," Bill
admitted, narrowing his brows as the complex business problems he'd been contending with all week
crowded together in his mind. Glory didn't have any
background in the lumber industry, but since none of
his managers enjoyed talking to him, she might be the
only sounding board he was likely to find.

"The old man will probably roll over in his grave,
but one of my thoughts is to give our employees some
say over their own future." Detecting a flicker of interest in her eyes, which was greater than any reaction
he'd gotten from his own men, he continued, "Profit
sharing is a possibility. The company's in deep trouble, but if the workers have a voice in what's happen-
ing, it's my guess that they'll work a lot harder to keep
the business from going under. I think it's about time

McCann Lumber began operating in the twentieth century."

Bill had told Glory about the heated arguments he used to have with his father on the subject of labor rights, so she should've been delighted with the policy changes he claimed to be considering, but she couldn't help but think that even if he eventually *did* put such changes into action, his generosity had come a little late. She also found it a bit difficult to believe that anything would actually come of these progressive ideas. For all his high-minded talk, Bill hadn't stuck around long enough to follow through on any of his big ideas before. Maybe he *did* have more social conscience than his father, but if he'd truly cared as much as he'd said, he should've stayed on to fight the good fight in the first place. Since he hadn't, she'd concluded that he was much more like Big Will than he'd ever been willing to admit, caring much more for himself than for other people.

That opinion was reflected in her next question. "Who would've thought that a self-serving McCann would see the advantages in profit sharing. Are you actually considering spreading a little of your accumulated wealth among the masses? Kenny told me the situation at the mill was bad, but he didn't say it was *that* desperate."

Bill lifted his eyebrows in startled surprise at her attack. "Who would've thought that an altruistic Hubbard could sound so sarcastic?"

Glory felt the warmth in her cheeks, but she met his eyes squarely. "A touch of cynicism is only one of the changes you're likely to notice in me, William Daniel McCann II. There are plenty of others."

"Such as?"

"Such as I've taken off my rose-colored glasses so I can view the real world. Now, instead of only seeing what I'd like to see, I can see what some people are really like."

"Some people . . . meaning me?"

Glory attempted a dismissive shrug, but Will wasn't fooled and she knew it. "I know now that you don't ride a white charger," she conceded reluctantly.

Bill frowned as he considered that statement along with everything else she'd just said. Beginning to think that she blamed him for much more than his desertion of her, he persisted, "I never pretended to be Prince Charming, Glory, but that doesn't mean I'm a complete villain, either."

"I didn't say you're a villain."

"You didn't have to say it, but that's what you think. Isn't it?" When Glory remained silent, he demanded, "Isn't it?"

Glory had spent ten long years building up a strong case against him, but even she was astonished by the depth of bitterness in her tone as she described the decline of his father and therefore, Hillsborough, after Bill had walked out on them both. As the accusing words fell from her mouth, she felt as if she were ridding herself of a long-festering poison. "What I think is that you're a chip right off the old block and that's why you and Big Will never got along. Neither one of you were ever capable of seeing beyond yourselves to the needs of other people. As long as you got what you wanted, you didn't give a damn about the other guy, not even if he was a member of your own family."

"Or the woman he claimed to love." Bill included the accusation that Glory couldn't bring herself to say, but once that truth was out in the open, she didn't hold back anything.

"Your pretty promises to me were worthless, just as worthless as the promises your daddy made to the people who worked for him. Unfortunately, none of them could afford to run away from their problems the way you did. They had to stay here and make the best of whatever Big Will felt inclined to offer, which for every year you were gone became less."

Unaware of the devastating effect her venom had on the man seated next to her, Glory finished her diatribe. "There's hardly a person in town who hasn't been at the mercy of the McCann's at one time or another. Well, I refuse to put myself in that position ever again!"

Bill stared at her in silence for a long time, but the look in his dark eyes told her just how furious she'd made him. Then, she saw something else. She saw a deep, soul-searing pain, and the hot flush of anger drained swiftly from her face.

"Maybe...it's not...right to blame you for *all* that's happened here," she admitted haltingly. "To compare you to Big Will, but—"

"But you do." Bill finished her sentence for her harshly. As the words faded she watched him withdraw from her, both physically and emotionally. "I think I hear Jamie."

"Bill!" Glory called after him, but he wasn't choosing to listen, and five minutes later she stood on the porch and watched him and his sleepy young son drive down the road. As the speeding pickup disappeared in a cloud of dust, Glory felt an agonizing wrench in her chest, as if she'd just cut out a piece of her own heart.

"How could I have been so spiteful?" she whispered wretchedly, but if she were totally honest with herself, she already knew why. An eye for an eye and a tooth for a tooth was the unwritten law of the hill country. In retribution for the hurt he'd once caused her, she'd gone against her own gentler nature and embraced that ruthless code. A long-awaited vengeance was hers, but Glory didn't feel any of the pleasure that she'd so often imagined for herself.

As it had always been from the time they'd been young children, Billy's pain was her pain, and by lashing out at him, she'd also hurt herself. For the first time since his return, she allowed herself to think about the possibility of their being together again, in body this time, as well as in spirit. Unfortunately, even though she might now be willing to entertain that idea, she'd just destroyed any chance that he would ever take her up on the offer.

Five

When the whistle proclaimed the end of the work day, Bill dropped the production report he was reading and stood up from his desk. Turning his back on the glass wall that fronted his spacious office, he stared out the rear window, which enabled him to view the gated entrances to both the lumberyard and mill and the mountains behind him. As the seconds ticked by, his frustration increased.

He might not be able to see them, but he could certainly feel all those mistrustful eyes boring into his back as his less-than-loyal employees filed down the long central hallway on their way out of the building. It normally took them about ten minutes to clear out, and Bill passed the time by recalling the day when his daddy had installed this big picture window and replaced the panelled walls of his office with glass. He also remembered what had motivated the remodeling.

"If a man is king of all he surveys, he'd best make sure he has a wide enough view," Big Will had joked to his ten-year-old son while leaning back in his leather chair and puffing on his favorite brand of Havana cigar. "Now that I can see those dang time clocks down by the gates, any laggarts will be paying me the price for clocking in late, and with my eye on 'em, I won't be having any shirkers up here in the office no more, either. When the time comes for you to sit in this chair, remember what I just told you and you won't have a speck of trouble being boss."

Big Will had enjoyed placing himself in a position to spy on his employees at work, but Bill felt as though he was the one on display, viewed from the other side of the glass as if he were some large, unknown species of insect trapped inside a specimen jar. Everyone who walked by his office peered in at him. For the first week or so, it was as if they were trying to decide if the bug they'd caught for themselves was really poisonous or just a harmless pest with an annoying sting and a very loud, obnoxious buzz. Since he'd been taking bites out of people for the past month, Bill could guess what decision they'd finally arrived at, but even knowing he could reach out of the jar at any time and haul any one of them inside with him, they still kept taking the risk.

For a moment, Bill thought the loud buzzing he heard was in his imagination, but then he realized that it was coming from his intercom, a hopelessly outdated piece of equipment that went along with everything else in this run-down den of antiquity. Even his secretary reminded him of a female Methuselah. Unfortunately, respecting his elders had been pounded into him at such an early age that he couldn't seem to work up the courage to fire Miss Peabody's arthritic bones.

Using the finger that most closely identified with his feelings, he stabbed down on the only key that still worked on the stupid machine. He didn't bother looking outside his office at the first and largest desk in a long row. Within an hour after his arrival in the building, the ancient woman who sat behind that head desk had informed him that she didn't answer to black scowls or erratic arm gestures. If he wanted her for something, he would have to follow proper procedure.

"What is it, Miss Peabody?"

"It's after office hours, but Kenneth Hubbard says he needs to see you, young Will. Shall I send him in or tell him to wait until morning?"

Bill had tried every way he could think of to keep the woman from referring to him by that childish name. He felt it undermined his still shaky authority, but in her book, anyone under the age of fifty was too wet behind the ears to rate much respect. In a long-suffering tone, he reminded her again. "I'd prefer it if you'd call me Bill, Miss Peabody, and I'm Mr. McCann to anyone who hasn't earned the right to call me by my first name. With that understanding, please allow Ken to proceed into my office."

The woman's sniff was audible, as were her pithy comments to his upcoming visitor. "That boy's got the miseries on him. Been as persnickety as they come all week. A good dose of castor oil would take care of the constriction in his bowels, but after the rude way he just spoke to me, I won't be the one to tell him. Since he put you in charge of keeping those cantankerous gents at Sugarbush Grocers happy, maybe you should do the honors."

Ken's lips were clamped tightly together as he strolled into Bill's office a minute later. He'd had enough dealings with the blue-haired dragonlady to know better than to laugh at anything she had to say, but he'd also suffered through enough staff meetings with William McCann II to fear what might happen if he so much as smiled at his employer's expense. He'd tried to explain to the sisters that this wasn't such a good idea, but then, he couldn't stand up to those three any better than Bill could lambaste his daddy's creaky old secretary.

"I know it's been one hell of a week," Ken began, but Bill gestured him to silence, then nodded out the window. Back straight as a poker, Miss Mildred Peabody was clutching her purse to her starched bosom and marching down the hall as quickly as her geriatric legs would carry her.

As soon as the woman was out of sight, Bill slumped down in his desk chair, propping his aching head up with one hand. "I realize I'm not the nicest guy in the world, but what did I ever do to deserve her? I swear, if you hadn't been here, she'd have marched into this office and boxed my ears for me."

If he hadn't heard the self-derisive humor behind that complaint, Ken might have managed to keep a straight face, but since he was a fellow sufferer when it came to dealing with touchy elderly women, he had to chuckle. "Then you owe me one, boss, cuz if I don't bring you over to the house for supper tonight, that's exactly what's gonna happen to me. Only in triplicate!''

Bill lifted his head off his hand, surprised by the invitation. Of all the men he had working under him, Glory's oldest brother had shown the most willingness to cooperate with his progressive ideas, but the man had never shown any indication that he remembered the fact that they'd once been friends. He'd assumed that Ken's distant attitude came as a result of Glory's perception of his desertion, and, after the royal dressing-down she'd recently given him, he'd also assumed that her entire family blamed him for the town's ills. Apparently he was wrong about that, or at least the Hubbard sisters didn't share those feelings, which he realized was highly possible, since the three dear old ladies had always taken kindly to him, even when he'd been at his worst. Ever since the long ago summer when Glory had dragged him home with her to meet her brothers, the sisters had behaved as if he were another one of their own.

"Are you agreeable to the asking, Ken?" he questioned dubiously. "Or just afraid of what will happen if you don't follow orders?"

Ken recognized a double-edged question when he heard one, but he was going to take a big chance and answer honestly. Unlike most other people in town over the past few weeks he'd revised his opinion about Big Will's "blue-blooded" baby boy. After watching the man work, he'd developed a grudging respect for him, even if some of his strong-arm methods reminded most folks of his daddy.

Maybe it was because he'd known and liked Bill as a young boy that Ken was willing to believe that those folks might be wrong. Ken was almost positive that unlike Big Will, by looking out for the company, the son wasn't just looking out for himself. He was trying to save them all. "I'm agreeable, though you might not get such a warm welcome from Zeke or David," he admitted. "Especially David. He's been out of work for close to a year now and had to move back in with the aunts. Zeke's not making much money working part-time for Zander's Plywood, but he's still self-supportin'."

Bill nodded in grim-faced understanding, thinking how ironic life could be at times. Glory didn't know it, but ten years ago, in exchange for the Hubbard boys' keeping their jobs at the mill, he'd agreed to stop seeing their little sister, and now she was the one accusing him of being responsible for David and Zeke's long-term unemployment. In Glory's estimation, Big Will's loss of interest in the company was a direct result of his son's having run off.

Adding insult to injury, even though he now had the power to put her brothers back on the payroll, he couldn't do it. In his current position, no matter how much he desired their beautiful sister, it wouldn't be fair to put the needs of two men before the needs of the company.

"Wish I could say they could come back to work in the next few days, but I won't be opening up a new field unless we get that contract with J & R Shipping for their containers. Until we're required to produce more than five million tons of paper annually, we don't need to hire on more loggers."

"I know," Ken replied. "But we're going to get that contract, and adding that onto the brown bags we're producing for the Sugarbush people, we'll be back in the black in no time."

Since that comment was the first truly positive statement he'd heard from any of his top managers, Bill wasn't certain he'd heard right. Reading his incredulous look correctly, Kenny hunched his shoulders and grimaced. "It's not that we're not behind you, boss," he tried to explain. "It's just that we've learned not to put too much faith in the decisions that are made out of this office. For some of us, trusting you will take a while, but if you keep pushing full steam ahead like you've been doing, mark my words, it'll come."

"Full steam ahead," Bill echoed hollowly, his despondent sigh fulminating evidence of his bone-weary exhaustion. The circles under his eyes indicated how many sleepless nights he'd endured over the last month reading every book on forest management that he could lay his hands on. The deep furrows in his brows were the result of the tension he was under to make sound business decisions.

During his summer breaks from the academy, his daddy had taught him everything he thought a mill owner should know, but after taking over the company, Bill had quickly discovered that he didn't understand nearly enough. He had no intention of following in Big Will's footsteps, but that meant he had to forge new paths through unknown territory. The school of hard knocks he'd attended in recent years had taught him plenty about being a "have not" instead of a "have," but when it came to running his own business, he was beginning to realize that he had a whole lot left to learn.

He was smart enough to figure out that men like Ken, who'd worked at McCann for many years, were a wealth of information, but extracting it from them was like pulling teeth. To stay on top of the situation himself, Bill hadn't put in less than sixteen hours a day since his first week on the job, and he didn't see any letup in sight. If things worked out right, over the next few weeks he would have two more lucrative contracts under his belt, but he couldn't afford to place all of his eggs in only two baskets, no matter how cushy their linings. Until he'd signed up enough accounts to guarantee another full year's worth of work, he couldn't stop pushing for the next sale. Until then, he didn't dare let up on himself or the people who worked for him.

At the same time as he struggled to overcome his sales problems, he had to work out a deal with the banks to finance the new manufacturing equipment that was going to be necessary once they stepped up production. The union boss was already causing him grief about the long hours his people were expected to work for unsatisfactory wages, while the office staff was covering their behinds with so much paper, they could easily supply a million-dollar account themselves.

On top of that, his field bosses were lecturing him about the sorry condition of his seed forests, and he still hadn't made up his mind whether to clear-cut his trees, risking fire and erosion, or if he should switch to a more selective system of cutting, which was less traumatic to the life of a forest.

Hell! For the last two weeks, he hadn't even had the time to sit down to a meal with his own son. "It was kind of your aunts to invite me, Hubbard, but I'm afraid I'll have to turn them down this time. I've skipped too many meals lately, and I know my boy is counting on me to show up at the table tonight. I spoke to Ida May around noon, and she made me promise to be there."

"That goes to show you just how quickly a man's plans can change once a bunch of old biddies stick their heads together."

"Huh?"

"Jamie's already over at the house," Ken informed him. "Cousin Ida asked Glory to bring him in with her from day care."

That news surprised the daylights out of Bill. "Your sister agreed to go that far out of her way to pick up my son?"

"She didn't have to go out of her way at all. Since the boy's right there anyway, she just walked him over to the house."

"Right where?" Bill asked. "Walked him over from where?"

Ken seemed confused by the questions, but once he'd replied to them, Bill was the one who didn't know what the hell was going on.

"From day care," Ken said, but when that only increased the intensity of Bill's frown, he hastened to add, "Ida May would've picked him up early like she usually does, but the sisters asked her if she'd make that special glaze of hers for the ham."

"What do you mean, Ida usually picks him up early?" Bill shouted vehemently.

Taken aback by the man's agitation, Ken threw up his hands defensively. "Listen, boss, if you've got a problem with your boy's babysitting schedule, don't lay into me. All I know is that the day shift gets over at five, and Glory says most of the other parents are done retrieving their kids by five-thirty. If you want your boy to stay on much later than that, he wouldn't have anyone much to play with besides Glory. Of course, she probably wouldn't mind since she rarely budges her stubborn tail out of that place much before the sun goes down, anyway."

It took him a while, but Bill finally managed to digest the unpalatable platter of information he'd just been handed. Without his knowledge or permission, the self-proclaimed Florence Nightingale of Jessup County had dispatched herself on another mission of mercy. Only this time she was going to discover that she'd overstepped her bounds. When it came to the welfare of his son, he alone made the decisions, and once he got done chewing her out, little Miss Do-gooder would be lucky if she didn't find a few fingers missing on her helping hand.

Through clenched teeth, Bill asked, "Okay, Hubbard, what time are we expected for dinner?"

"In honor of your coming, *supper*," Ken said, emphasizing the proper word in a kindly attempt to remind the man that he was back in a small town. "The sisters have delayed serving until six-thirty."

Bill made note of the correction with a wry smile, well aware that if he was ever going to be fully accepted by these people, he was going to have to start playing by the local rules. "What time does your family normally eat?"

"Unless there's company invited, everyone is expected at the table at six o'clock on the dot or they can just make do without their vittles. Course, since the aunts feel that Glory is doing the Lord's work, she's excused more often than not. They spoil that girl something awful, and always have."

Where Glory was concerned, Bill was spoiling for something, too, but Ken didn't need to know what action he intended to take with the resident angel of mercy. He glanced at his watch and promptly stood up. "Then we'd better get a move on."

Allowing Ken to proceed him through the door, Bill lifted his suitcoat off its hook on the wall, then flicked off the lights. "I didn't realize that you and Liliah shared a house with the sisters."

"We don't," Ken informed him, wondering how it was that rich folk knew so little about the less-advantaged, while lesser folks knew most everything there was to know about the rich. Why, he could even tell Bill how many eggs he liked for his breakfast and that he preferred his coffee with plenty of sugar. "We have a place over on Main Street, but that doesn't mean we're excused from Friday-night supper with the aunts. Let me tell you, any Hubbard, young or old, that doesn't make it over there had best have a very good reason or they won't hear the end of it."

Bill had never thought to ask before, but since Ken was well into his thirties by now, he probably had several children. "Do you and your wife have a big family?"

Ken's blue eyes twinkled. "Had some trouble getting started, but once they commenced to arriving, our young'ns came by twos. The eight-year-old girls are sweet-tempered, but our six-year-old boys are a twin-pack of trouble.''

Bill grinned. ''If I remember correctly, you and your three brothers were considered by some to be quite a handful for those three dear old ladies to handle.''

Kenny shot him a look that took them both back a lot of years. ''And there were plenty of others around who thought no one alive could handle you.''

''Even so, I remember being invited to a few Sunday dinners at your house the summer before I left for the academy,'' Bill recalled fondly. ''One hour after church services and not a minute later. What happened? Did they switch days on you?''

''Nope, there's always Sunday dinner.''

''What does Liliah have to say about that?'' Bill asked curiously, nodding to the security guard who was just signing in as he and Ken walked out of the building.

Ken shrugged. ''What is there to say? Family's family, and hers has near as many quirks as mine. One time, she and I went away for the weekend without telling her momma, and when we got back, the woman had checked herself in at the community hospital.''

''What for!''

''Told us she was so beside herself with worry, she'd like on to die. The doctor on duty could've sworn that she was near enough to death's door to catch sight of Saint Peter. The woman didn't rally herself until Liliah and me knelt down beside her deathbed and begged for forgiveness.''

Bill had often tried to imagine what being connected to a loving family would be like. From the time Glory had dragged him home to meet her kin, he'd envied the closeness she enjoyed with her brothers and aunts and all the other members of the large Hubbard clan. After hearing what Ken had to endure in order to keep peace among his relatives, Bill had to wonder if being an only child had really been so bad. Maybe he'd missed out on a lot as a kid, but at this point in his life, he'd been on his own far too long to appreciate somebody else telling him where he could go or what he could do.

On the other hand, he acknowledged bitterly, a man's needs were entirely different than a boy's. A man could make it on his own, whereas a boy couldn't. A boy needed constant reassurance that he was loved. For that reason, Bill had never quite forgiven his mother for giving up on her efforts to civilize him and shipping him off to military school when he was nine.

After that neither one of his parents had much cared what he did or where he went during the school term as long as they didn't have to deal with his bad behavior while he was gone. To make sure they weren't contacted, they'd donated enough money to the academy to build a new gymnasium, a library as big as the nearest university's and enough whitewash to have even the most outrageous of his boyhood schemes dealt with as harmless pranks. It hadn't taken him long to figure out that his presence was only tolerated at home for a few months during the summer because, as their sole heir, it was necessary for him to learn how to run the family business. If that hadn't been the case they probably would've kept him at school the entire year-round.

Resenting their unfeeling attitude, he'd tried every-thing he could think of to claim their full attention, but eventually he'd learned that nothing he did was ever too black for the headmaster to cover up. That is, not until he'd reached his last term.

Of course, the method he'd finally used to get him-self expelled wouldn't have worked for him much ear-lier. That was the year he'd started putting on extra muscle by lifting weights, and not too long after that the headmaster had concluded that the reputation of his fair-haired daughter was far more important to him than the mental well-being of the school's largest benefactor.

It wasn't until he was back home in Hillsborough that Bill had realized that he'd accomplished nothing by getting thrown out of school. Maybe if his momma had still been alive she would've cared enough, at least for appearances sake, to chastise him for sacrificing his education and leading a "nice" girl astray, but she'd died of cancer the previous spring. As for his daddy, Big Will had been amused by the whole affair, excusing his son's romantic misdeeds with a boys-will-be-boys attitude that had finally made it clear to Bill that he would never be expected to follow the same rules as the rest of society.

"I sowed plenty of wild oats when I was your age and plenty more after, but your momma knew enough to turn a blind eye when necessary. She liked the niceties I could give her much more than she disliked my wanderin' eye," Big Will had boasted. "But just you remember that a McCann don't marry white trash, so keep your pants zipped around here. If you need that kind of satisfaction I'll give you the cash to pay for the type of woman that won't show up pregnant on our doorstep expectin' you to do right by her.''

After delivering that ''loving'' paternal speech, he'd pulled a piece of paper out of his pocket and handed it over to Bill. ''I got Principal Crowley to make out this here diploma for you. I never put much store in education, but your mamma had her heart set on you graduating from high school and going to college. If that's what you plan to do, it's fine by me. Go pick yourself out a good school and I'll pay the right folks to get you in. Otherwise, come fall, you can take up your rightful place at the mill.''

Your rightful place at the mill. Those fateful words echoed and re-echoed inside Bill's head. Ever since he'd come back to this godforsaken town, his dreams had been filled with the triumphant sound of Big Will McCann's laughter rising up from the grave. Come hell or high water, even though he'd had to die in order to do it, the old man had finally gotten his way.

Six

___

For once in her life, Glory was grateful that her position in the family placed her closest to the children who occupied the foot of the long table. Since, as the guest of honor, Bill was seated at the head, his piercing gaze had to pass through at least eight other people before it reached her. Which wasn't to say she hadn't been struck a few times since the meal began, Glory acknowledged glumly, using her fork to push the uneaten food around on her plate.

Knowing she was the target of Bill's poisonous visual darts, Glory was forced to admit that she'd jumped to some very wrong conclusions about tonight's occasion. Bill's acceptance of her aunts' invitation hadn't been due to any friendly feelings he still harbored toward her. The man might have enrolled his son in her day-care program, but just because he considered her a qualified baby-sitter, she'd been foolish to assume that he'd forgiven her for all the hateful things she'd said to him the last time they'd met.

As soon as he'd walked through the door this evening and spotted her seated on the floor in the living room, playing dominos with Jamie, she'd immediately been given to understand that in the days since their last confrontation he'd thought of several things he would like to say to her in return, none of which were going to be pleasant.

Luckily, her aunts had swooped down upon him before he'd taken too many more steps inside their house, so thus far he'd been denied the opportunity to vent his spleen, but Glory didn't doubt that he would eventually find a way to get to her. Considering the pent-up anger she'd sensed in him, she was surprised that he'd waited this long for a showdown. Then, after noting the dark circles under his eyes, the unhealthy color of his complexion and the grooves of tension around his mouth, she'd realized what had prompted the delay. The poor man looked as if he hadn't slept a wink in days.

None of her brothers ever noticed such things, but all it had taken was one glance for every woman in the room to know that their guest was on his last legs. In the Hubbard house, exhausted males were overwhelmed by kindness, and though after all these years William Daniel McCann II was practically a stranger to them, the aunts still had a soft spot in their hearts for the boy he'd once been. If Glory hadn't felt so threatened by the antagonistic expression in his eyes when he'd first spotted her, she would've laughed at the incredulous expression on Bill's face when he'd found himself surrounded by the clucking flock of elderly women.

Like brooding hens with an ailing young rooster, the Hubbard sisters and Cousin Ida had hovered around him, quickly easing him out of his rumpled gray suit-coat and navy-blue tie, then whisking him across the hall into the dining room. Aunt Ophelia had sent a warning glance over her shoulder at David and Zeke, and any surliness those two might have been harboring for the weary man in her protective charge was immediately squelched. Aunt Carrie had pulled out the head chair at the table, the overstuffed one with two armrests, and bade him to sit down, while Aunt Winnie had quickly directed the remainder of the Hubbard flock into their assigned places.

The sooner everyone sat down, the sooner Bill could take in nourishment, and Glory had learned long ago that the aunts firmly believed that food in great quantities was the best cure for exhaustion. As the meal progressed, Bill had been besieged by helpful female hands filling his plate with a mountain of food and keeping it filled while he struggled politely to make a small dent in what was there before he was given seconds and thirds. His water glass was never allowed to go empty. His coffee cup was always filled to the brim. He dropped a fork and had it replaced a second after it had hit the floor.

When it was time for dessert, Glory risked a peek around her brother David's broad shoulder and under Zeke's arm. To her relief, she saw that her aunts and Cousin Ida had accomplished what most men wouldn't dare try. The most powerful cock in Hills-borough didn't have enough strength left to crow in protest, even when his supper plate was replaced with one that contained two large pieces of apple pie topped with several scoops of homemade vanilla ice cream.

If indigestion worked in her favor, Glory figured that once the meal was officially over, he would be so anxious to escape the fluttering hens in this overcrowded coop that he would forget all about the nervous young chick who'd hidden herself away from him farther down on the roost. As she watched him force down his dessert, she decided she had it made.

A few minutes later, however, Glory discovered that there was a fox in the hen house. Before her brothers had filed away from the table to watch television and the children gone out to the back porch to play board games, before Glory could make good her escape into the kitchen, Kenny's wife, Liliah, a sneaky, green-eyed vixen who up until tonight Glory had looked upon as one of her dearest friends, snuck up behind her chair and routed her right off her safe perch.

"There's no need for you to help out with the dishes tonight. We've more than enough hands," Liliah assured, patting Glory on the shoulder as she nodded graciously at Bill. "I understand there's some problem with Jamie's day-care attendance that you need to speak with his daddy about."

Since Jamie was happy as a clam at day care, Glory didn't buy that excuse for a minute, and her hackles rose at Bill's nasty choice of tactics. Apparently he was hellbent on having it out with her tonight, but he didn't have to malign her work in order to do it and her resentful expression told him so. "Oh? What sort of problem would that be?"

"A major one," Bill growled, rolling up his shirt sleeves as he pushed back his chair.

Both women interpreted his action as a preparation for battle, and Liliah glanced at Glory in startled surprise. Then, in another abortive attempt to be helpful, the woman hastened to suggest, "With all of us here, it's so blamed noisy in the house. I think it might be a good idea if you two went outside to talk this over. I'll be glad to keep an eye on Jamie until you get back."

Bill's reply was immediate. "I think that's a very good idea."

Suppressing a groan, Glory resigned herself to her fate, but she wasn't above delaying it for as long as possible. She took her time getting up from the table, swallowing the last droplets of water in her glass and carefully stacking her used dishes and silverware. Once standing, she began gathering up the soiled napkins on her side of the table into a neat pile.

Anyone would be cowed by Bill's obvious hostility, but Glory found some solace in the sickly tinge she noticed beneath his skin. Considering the amount of food he'd just packed away, odds were that he would hit fast and hard, then run off for the antacid. Since every moment of delay was time in her favor, she stated innocently, "I'll be ready to go as soon as I carry a load of these dirty dishes into the kitchen."

"Well, I'm ready now," Bill snapped, bringing an end to Glory's stalling by rounding the table and grasping her firmly by the elbow. "This shouldn't take us more than a few minutes."

"Take all the time you need," Liliah offered, but Bill had Glory out the front door and down the steps so fast, Glory doubted he'd heard. She hoped not, for she'd suffered through quite enough of Liliah's kind offers for one day.

She didn't complain, however, until she was half dragged around the side of the house. "Do you mind!"

"Not in the least," Bill replied unfeelingly and kept right on walking.

His grip on her arm was like steel, so Glory had no choice but to keep up with his long-legged stride, and by the time he'd hauled her with him into the back-yard, she was breathing like a winded race horse. She thought he would stop once they reached the small gazebo at the rear of the property, but evidently he was afraid his voice might carry too well even from that distance, so he continued on at the same unrelenting pace.

After covering a few more yards, Glory again attempted to free her arm, but Bill refused to relinquish it until they were deep inside the thick pine grove that bordered the acreage behind her aunts' house. For a moment the fragrant scent of evergreen overwhelmed her with the memory of another small wood, where as a young girl she'd been kissed for the very first time. She remembered how tender that kiss had been, how gentle the hands that cradled her head, but that joyful recollection was quickly vanquished as Bill thrust her arm away from him.

Hands on hips, he glared down at her and demanded, "Okay, lady, explain what gives you the right to make decisions about my son without consulting me?"

Prepared to be lambasted for judging his past actions so harshly, Glory blinked at the unexpected line of attack. Then, when he added nothing more to the question, she realized that Bill really *did* have some problem with how she was doing her job. She didn't know whether she was relieved by that knowledge or not, especially since she had no idea what decisions he could possibly be talking about.

As far as Jamie was concerned, the only decisions she made were over his lunch menu and which of the many varied activities offered in her day-care program would be best suited for his age and maturity. Up until now, no parent had ever questioned her judgment concerning balanced meals or had expected her to ask for their permission for their child to take part in a rousing game of freeze tag. Judging by his thundercloud expression, she doubted that Bill was referring to anything so inconsequential.

"Would you mind qualifying that a bit?" she suggested, doing her best to ignore the fact that he appeared about ready to strangle her.

"Seems like a pretty straightforward question to me," he bit out sarcastically. "But then, considering your exalted position in this one-horse town, I imagine that you're rarely called to answer for your transgressions. Well guess what, sweetheart? I don't give a damn about your lofty intentions. If I wanted my son looked after by you, I would have enrolled him in your program myself!"

Glory's mouth dropped open and her brows went up. "Didn't you?"

"Didn't I what?"

"Enroll him yourself?"

"You know damned well I didn't! You took it upon yourself to decide what's best for my kid, and I want to tell you right now, that—"

"I did no such thing," Glory defended herself. "When Ida May brought him down to the center, I assumed that you had approved of the idea, especially since she told me all about the long hours you've been keeping and how lonely Jamie was all day up on that mountain with nothing to do and no one to play with."

"Well, you assumed wrong," Bill retorted, but with far less bluster than before. Glory's gibe about Jamie's loneliness really hit him where it hurt, and he felt guilty, just as he was sure she'd intended him to feel. "As far as I knew, Jamie was in Ida's care, not yours."

Glory stared at him for a few moments in offended silence, then saw something in his expression that altered her tone of voice. "Ida May might be a good housekeeper, but you of all people should know that she'd never had much time for kids," she reminded him gently. "Considering how busy you've been at the mill, she was probably reluctant to bother you with something she could take care of so easily herself."

"I guess so," Bill agreed, feeling more deflated by the second.

"I'm sure if she knew how you felt about me, she would have made other arrangements for Jamie. Please don't blame her for that."

"I don't blame her."

Glory sighed. "You blame me."

"I'm not blaming either one of you!"

"But you're still angry with me," Glory concluded unhappily, waiting for him to start blasting her with all the recriminations that she'd expected from him in the first place.

What the hell did he have to be angry with her about? Bill asked himself dejectedly. He was the one who was guilty of neglecting his child, not Glory. He was the one who'd allowed himself to forget what it had been like for him as a kid, locked away in that gray-stone fortress with no one for company but an overworked housekeeper. Ida May had neither the time nor the inclination to entertain rambunctious little boys, so she'd naturally turned to Gloria for help, and the two of them had worked out a solution that was beneficial for all concerned, including him.

"No, I'm not angry with you." Turning away from Glory, Bill jammed his hands into his pants pockets and stared up at the mountain that overlooked the town. Unaware of the bitter lines etched in his face and the defeated sag to his shoulders, he conceded, "Under the circumstances, Ida May was right to do what she did. I haven't had time for anything besides work lately... not even for Jamie. Like it or not, until I get the business turned around, I've got to count on other people to look after my son."

Glory followed his forlorn gaze up the towering mountain, and for the first time she began to sense the overwhelming weight Bill was presently carrying on his shoulders. From the conversations she'd heard here and there around town, she also knew that he was carrying it alone. Until he proved himself to be a better man than his father, no one was willing to trust him.

Bill didn't have to say what he was thinking. Glory already knew. They were both standing in the shadow of McCann Mountain, but he was also standing in the shadow of the man it was named after. "Since so many other people are counting on you, it's only fair that you should be able to count on them," she assured him.

"Fair?" Bill laughed contemptuously. "If you think life is fair, then you lied to me about taking off your rose-colored glasses."

"*I've* never lied to *you* about anything," Glory retorted, and the emphasis she placed on the personal pronouns made it clear to him that she believed he couldn't make the same claim.

Bill clenched his jaw to hold back a frustrated curse. "Sometimes a lie is kinder than the truth."

"But in the long run, the truth is easier to live with."

Bill switched his gaze back up the mountain to the truth he was forced to live with for the rest of his life. "The hell it is."

As usual, Glory was quick to tread on the heels of his thoughts. "You didn't have to volunteer to take over for Big Will. You could have sold out and moved on," she stated quietly, taking a step closer to him. "Why didn't you?"

Several moments passed and Glory didn't think he was going to answer. When he did, it wasn't the answer she was expecting, but one that made her realize just how much distance there was between them now—a cold empty space that her own vengeful words had created. "Why I stayed doesn't matter. The only thing that matters is whether or not I can make the damned thing work."

"And can you?"

She hadn't intended the question to sound like a vote of nonconfidence, but he'd obviously concluded that she was as big a doubting Thomas as everyone else in town. "I'm not planning to run out on everyone again, if that's what you're so concerned about," he snapped, his tone cutting. "If McCann goes down, I'll go down with it. Happy now?"

Glory ignored her own pain, for suddenly she was very much aware that his wounds went much deeper than hers and that most of them had been made long before he'd ever met her. As a young boy he hadn't been such an expert at hiding his emotions that she hadn't been able to tell when something was deeply troubling him. But apparently Bill McCann had acquired a lot of new skills while he'd been away.

In that respect, Glory was glad that she'd made him angry enough to let down his guard a little, otherwise she still wouldn't have realized that she wasn't the only one who was hurting. "I'd be a lot happier if you'll agree to accept my apology. I—I never should have said all those cruel things to you the other day."

"Why apologize? You meant them," Bill said, his eyes daring her to deny it.

"Half, maybe," she insisted stubbornly, trying not to shiver beneath his cold gaze. "Not all."

Admiring her nerve if not her honesty, Bill inquired, "Which half?"

Glory heard the slight warming in his tone, but knew if she gave him the specifics he asked for, they would be right back in the ice age. "The wrong half."

Bill hadn't had anything to smile about in days, but Glory's unsubtle hedging brought one to his lips. "I take it that you're leaving me to decide what part was wrong, which makes me think that you're a chicken."

"Funny you should say that," Glory replied, and relayed the hen house analogy she'd thought of over supper.

Seeing the parallel, Bill had to laugh—a genuine, full-fledged laugh. "If I hadn't missed so many meals lately, I probably would be feeling like one sorry rooster about now."

"I was hoping that a bile attack would save me from your wrath," Glory admitted, striving but failing to look guilty for wishing him ill.

Glory's spirits soared as Bill laughed again. "You and Miss Peabody," he said, disclosing the diagnosis his secretary had made about him to her brother that afternoon. "She suggested a strong dose of caster oil, but if that's what it's going to take, I think I'll stay constricted."

Encouraged by his amusement, Glory asked, "Remember the time we stole that big batch of chocolate fudge off the back porch and ate ourselves sick? Aunt Carrie dosed us with cod-liver oil, and that's much worse than castor."

Bill grinned at the memory. "Just the smell made me lose my cookies."

Glory groaned empathetically. "Ever since that day, I shy away from anything with chocolate."

"Even Aunt Winnie's chocolate-cream pie?"

Wincing, Glory conceded, "Well...maybe not Winnie's pie, but absolutely everything else."

"Aunt Ophelia's devil's-food cake?"

Glory scowled at him. "I wasn't referring to dark chocolate."

"Ah." Bill nodded his head sagely. "Then it's Aunt Carrie's chocolate supreme bars with the butter brickle inside and the peanut-butter frosting that you refuse to eat."

Glory threw up her hands. Bill had remembered every single one of her favorite desserts, and he'd also figured out that she would never pass up any one of them. "Okay! Okay, so I lied," she admitted, jutting out her chin. "Wanna make summp'in of it?"

"You bet," Bill retorted, but if she was expecting him to react to that challenge like he would've when they were kids, she was in for a surprise. Glory could stick her chin out as far as she could but he'd still see beyond it to her soft kissable mouth, and if she wanted him to see her as a child, she shouldn't be wearing that off-the-shoulder blouse and such well-fitting jeans. "But I'd probably get my face slapped if I tried."

Glory placed both her hands on her hips and cocked her head to one side. "Tried what?"

Smirking at her belligerent stance, Bill told her. "Kissing you...making love to you...doing everything in my bodily power to thank you for lifting my spirits and making me laugh."

Before she thought better of it, Glory went up on tiptoes and kissed him first, a tiny peck on the cheek. "No thanks are necessary."

"Maybe not in your opinion..." Bill's voice trailed off, but the liquid warmth in his dark violet eyes reinforced his contention that he possessed an opposing view.

Meeting that hot look, Glory could feel the desirous heat rush into her cheeks, and her lips parted breathlessly. Compelled by a force she couldn't control, she lifted her hand to his chest and lay her palm over his thudding heartbeat. "Would you laugh if I told you that the thought of your bodily power makes me say things that I don't mean?"

"No." Bill reached up and clasped her hand, holding it away from him. Then, before she could interpret the gesture as a rejection, he used his free hand to slowly, deliberately, unbutton his shirt. A few seconds later, Glory was touching bare skin, her fingers pressed against hard, bronzed muscle. "Not if it also makes you want to do things you're frightened of doing and feel things you've never felt before."

"I've always been afraid of the way you make me feel," Glory admitted huskily, feeling her own heart beginning to pound with the same rapid beat as the one she felt beneath her fingers. But Glory knew Bill's racing heartbeat wasn't the only thing that was making hers frantic. It was the animal heat of his skin, the soft, springy texture of his chest hair and the shocking awareness that her touch was making his nipple harden.

"I told you that you could do the same for me," he reminded her. "If you hadn't been so damned young and innocent back then, I would've made sure that you realized that about the male of the species, and a few other things, as well."

"What other things?" Glory asked, gasping in surprise when he wrapped his arm around her waist and pulled her against him. "Oh . . . th-those things," she stammered, as hip to hip and thigh to thigh, she was given a graphic example of the difference between female and male, soft and hard.

"Were you ever aware of how much I ached for you? After those nights in Hunter's Grove I had to take the long way home past the south creek so the whole damned town couldn't tell what I'd been up to in the woods."

Flushing, Glory lowered her gaze to his throat. "Of course I knew," she admitted, though he wasn't able to see the very pleased expression on her face. "I might have been a virgin, but I took sex education in school just like everyone else."

"According to that blush, you're still a virgin."

There were times, Glory thought, when it was more comfortable to lie, but after spouting that platitude to Bill about truth being easier to live with, she didn't dare continue the only deception she'd ever attempted around him. "So I am," she conceded peevishly. "Happy now?"

Bill's laugh was supremely male and incredibly sexy. "I'd be a lot happier if you'd agree to accept me as the man who alleviates your condition."

He expected the blush, but neither the serene smile nor the tart admonishment. "It's about time you got around to taking me up on what, if you recall, was originally *my* offer, William McCann. Ten long years is enough for any normal, red-blooded American woman to wait."

Bill kissed her breathless, then assured, "I promise you, sweetheart. The waiting is over."

Seven

Bill hadn't exactly lived up to that promise. Glory had been kept waiting for well over two hours before she finally heard a car drive up. Like a scalded cat, she jumped off the couch and ran to the mirror, making certain that her hair wasn't messed up and that her lipstick was still on straight. While she'd waited for Bill to arrive, she'd changed clothes three times, having no idea what was proper for a woman to wear when she greeted her prospective lover. Getting all gussied up in a dress and high heels seemed silly, but shorts and a top didn't seem quite right, either, and she didn't even own a sexy negligee.

Eventually, she'd opted for the white jeans that emphasized her tiny waist and slender hips, but then she'd covered them both with an oversize T-shirt. It had taken every speck of her rapidly dwindling courage, but she'd left off her bra, which she quickly discovered had turned out to be a very bad idea. Every time she heard a car passing on the road, her nipples tightened to erect points that were shamelessly visible beneath the soft cotton.

She'd almost made up her mind to put her bra back on, but then she'd heard the crunch of tires on the loose gravel of her drive and it was too late. Knowing he was expected, Bill just might walk right in, and the last thing she wanted was for him to catch her frantically putting more clothes on, especially when the purpose of his nocturnal visit was for the two of them to take off what was already there.

"Oh, lordy," Glory breathed, her stomach doing cartwheels as she contemplated what was supposed to happen afterward. Taking off their clothes was only the first step in the process toward total intimacy. Once that task was accomplished, Bill was going to take her to bed and touch her all over. Not only that, but he was going to expect her to do the same thing to him.

Glory clutched her churning stomach. "I'm going to be sick. I just know it."

As soon as those lily-livered words escaped her lips, Glory turned on herself in disgust. "Grow up, Hubbard! Or would you rather stay a virgin for another quarter of a century?"

Taking a deep, calming breath, Glory stepped outside onto the porch. The first thing she noted was that Bill had traded in his rattletrap pickup truck for Big Will's fancy Cadillac. She also saw that he was as anxious as she to prevent the whole town from buzzing about his late-night visit to her home, for instead of parking the easily recognizable car in full view of the road, he'd pulled in between the woodshed and the house. When he opened the door and slid out from behind the wheel, Glory suffered another knee-knocking attack of nerves.

"Okay, so I'm not as liberated as I thought," she muttered darkly to herself, folding her arms defensively across her chest as she watched his approach. "But I'm going to go through with this thing if it kills me!"

Unlike her, Bill certainly didn't look as if he were suffering from any second thoughts, Glory observed with a gulp, and according to the spring in his step, he'd also made a miraculous recovery from his previous exhaustion. Hands in his pockets, he walked with a leisurely stride, stretching his well-fit jeans against the powerful muscles of his thighs with each step. To add to his sexy appearance, he was wearing a long-sleeved blue chambray shirt rolled up to the elbows, and he'd left it unbuttoned.

Glory felt all trembly inside as she glimpsed the narrow expanse of burnished skin exposed by his open shirt, and her fingers tingled with the memory of how smooth and warm that skin had been to the touch. As she anticipated the time when she would be given free access to far more of his body than that which was already exposed to her gaze, several other parts of her body began to tingle. Glory tightened her already folded arms, trying to ease the heavy throbbing in her nipples.

Seeing where her anxious eyes were glued, Bill's opening comment was about the weather. "Hot night, isn't it?"

Glory grabbed at that excuse like a lifeline, lifting one hand to wave at her flushed cheeks. "And so humid that it's hard to breathe."

"Sorry I took so long," he apologized as he jumped up on the porch. "It took me a while to get Jamie settled down for the night. He had a great time with Kenny's kids tonight. And he seemed to fit right in."

"Why wouldn't he?" Glory asked.

"We've moved around a lot, so he hasn't spent much time around children his own age," Bill said, nodding to the porch swing. Glory took off for it as if she were shooting out of a starting box, and Bill lifted his hand over his mouth to hide his smile. She was wound up tighter than a drum, and to get her to relax was going to be quite a challenge. Of course, Bill had always enjoyed any challenge Glory offered him, and he knew that he was going to reap a spectacular reward by answering this one.

"I wouldn't feel guilty about that," Glory said, clutching the chains of the swing with one hand as Bill sat down beside her and pushed it into motion. "Jamie seems very well adjusted."

Bill heard the surprise in her voice and laughed without humor. "Which amazes you, considering who his father is."

"I didn't say that."

"You didn't have to say it, and I don't blame you for thinking it," he added, noting her chagrined expression. "At his age, I was a little monster, and most folks around here think I haven't changed a bit."

"I don't think you're a monster. At least, not a very big one," she amended, beginning to relax now that she realized Bill wasn't planning to pounce on her, strip off her clothes and drag her away to the bedroom in two minutes flat.

Bill grinned. "Gee, thanks."

Demonstrating the undeserved loyalty that had always warmed his lonely heart, Glory proceeded to excuse his bad behavior as a child. "You only acted up when you were Jamie's age because you were forced to contend with so many complex problems."

"In other words, I was pretty screwed up."

"You were hurt and confused," Glory corrected indignantly. "Jamie doesn't need to worry about whether or not he's loved, and with that kind of security, a child can adjust to most anything his parents do. Your folks never gave you that extremely essential assurance."

She shouldn't have brought up the subject of his parents, for they were the last thing Bill wanted to talk about tonight. He could see, however, that she was about to continue with her psychoanalysis of his childhood traumas, so he stopped her next words in a way that was guaranteed to lead her off in an entirely different direction. Leaning his head toward her, he whispered huskily in her ear. "You aren't wearing a bra, are you? That's the first thing I noticed when I got out of the car."

Glory swallowed, caught completely off guard. "You did?"

"Uh-huh," he replied softly, sliding his arm behind her back and pulling her close enough so that their thighs touched. Her body stiffened when he brought his hand beneath her arm and his knuckles brushed against the side of her left breast. Using his thumb, he stroked the soft curve beneath her thin shirt and felt her tremble. "Do your nipples throb?"

Glory didn't know if it was the power of suggestion, but suddenly both of her breasts felt terribly swollen and achy, the tips so aroused that she feared she might scream if his fingers so much as grazed them. She trembled in reaction to the thought, but Bill wasn't content with merely a verbal seduction, although his next question inveigled her into a delicious web of anticipation.

"I can soothe the throbbing if you want me to," he whispered, easing her shoulders around until her upper body was facing him. To insure that the position was comfortable, he reached over and lifted her legs, then set them down over his thighs. A second later Glory realized that they were commencing with the disrobing part of the agenda. Or at least she was, she amended, fighting down panic as Bill slowly pulled up her T-shirt, exposing her waist, her midriff, and then—

"Billy!" she protested in a strangled tone, but when he drew the shirt over her head and she felt the cool night air on her naked breasts, her throat closed up completely. As if that erotic stimulation wasn't enough, Bill cupped their weight in his palms, not pausing for her to recover from that shock before he lowered his head. He closed his mouth over one nipple, open and hot, his tongue tantalizing the swollen tip, and Glory cried out at the acute pleasure, instinctively arching her back to give him better access.

"That's it," he encouraged softly, bringing his arm behind her and bending her back over it as he switched his attention to her other breast. "Go with your feelings, Glory. Just relax, and let yourself go with it."

Relax! Glory had to bite her lip to keep from screaming as an unbearable tension built up inside her. He used his tongue to create the sweetest kind of ache she'd ever felt, but it wasn't only her breasts that were throbbing with exquisite feeling. She was throbbing all over, and when he drew her nipple deeply inside his mouth, she felt an answering heat deep inside her womb.

"Please, Billy...please," she pleaded, when the heat threatened to overwhelm her.

Bill knew exactly what she was begging for and he was happy to oblige her needs. With one smooth motion, he lifted her fully onto his lap, reveling for a moment in the feel of her small, tight bottom pressed against the throbbing evidence of his own desire, before standing up with her in his arms. As he carried her inside the house, his gaze moved possessively over her smooth, creamy breasts, taking supreme pleasure in the knowledge that his mouth had caused their tips to tighten so beguilingly.

"I want to see all of you . . . explore every beautiful inch with my hands and mouth," he murmured, his chest rising and falling with each ragged breath. "I've dreamed about making love with you so many times, ever since that last night at Hunter's Grove when I had to deny myself the pleasure of having you. That was the hardest thing I've ever had to do in my life. I thought you were the most beautiful thing I'd ever seen, but you're even more beautiful now than you were back then."

"I was yours for the taking," Glory reminded him, confused by his version of the story. "If you wanted me so badly, why did you reject me like that?"

Bill had no intention of ruining the mood he'd just created by reintroducing the topic he most hated to talk about. For once, Big Will wasn't going to come between him and what he wanted. Tonight, he would banish all thoughts of that black-hearted tyrant from his mind. "You were only sixteen then, Glory, and you deserved better than anything I had to offer you."

"I would've been willing to take whatever you had to give," Glory informed him honestly.

"I know," Bill replied, then forestalled further talk by bending to her mouth.

He brought his lips to hers and opened them with enticing strokes of his tongue. When they parted for him, his tongue penetrated, and Glory closed her eyes with a hungry moan. His kiss made the blood rage in her veins, but she wanted so much more from him. She wanted to feel the crush of his body on hers, to be burned by the heat of his naked skin. She wanted the fulfillment of his possession, to be part of him, to love him with the wild passion that surged through her body and to feel that passion returned.

"Walk faster, Billy," she pleaded desperately when he finally ended the kiss, and Bill chuckled low in his throat as he shouldered open the door to her softly lit bedroom.

Once inside, he drew down the spread and placed her carefully between the white sheets on the four-poster bed, making her blush when he folded back the edge of her floral coverlet and held it next to one of her nipples, his appreciative eyes comparing design patterns. "I bet these delicate buds don't taste as good as yours," he ventured, smiling indulgently as her face went scarlet to the roots of her hair.

"I wish you wouldn't say things like that! It embarrasses me."

"Sorry," Bill apologized, but he didn't look very contrite as he let go of the bedspread and stood back. "It's just that you look so damned pretty in that color." His eyes roamed from one glowing mound to the other. "All-over pink."

"Oh!" Glory exclaimed, scrambling up on her knees and grabbing for a pillow to hide the naked curves he was so blatantly admiring. "You're deliberately trying to make me blush."

Bill didn't bother to deny it. "Finding a woman who still can is delightfully refreshing, and knowing I can make your skin glow with just a few well-chosen words drives me crazy. But then, glowing skin is only one of a number of reactions I enjoy inspiring in you. For instance, making your breasts swell with my mouth gives me just as much pleasure."

He watched her face brighten even more, knowing exactly how she would react to such blatant teasing. He also knew that he could expect to see that fiery color intensify the instant she saw him minus his clothes. Since she was already blushing, however, when the moment of truth actually did arrive, she would be able to retain at least some of her feminine dignity. She might be a virgin, but she was also twenty-five years old, and it was his guess that she wouldn't want him to see how embarrassed she was when confronted by a completely aroused naked man.

Glory could hardly breathe as Bill moved back a few feet from the bed, stepped out of his loafers and shrugged out of his shirt. She couldn't take her eyes off him, fascinated by the rippling play of deeply tanned muscles as he tossed the shirt over his shoulder. When he brought his hands to the zipper of his jeans and pulled downward, her eyes followed the tantalizing line of dark curling hair until it disappeared beneath the low-slung waistband of his white briefs. When the jeans came off, the briefs went with them, and then he was moving swiftly forward—too swiftly.

"Stop!" she cried, throwing up one hand in protest.

"Glory..." Bill began, in a tone meant to soothe her fears. Concentrating on his face, she didn't see him slide a small packet between the sheets, which, considering her current level of anxiety, he assumed would only have made matters worse. "Just lie back and relax. I realize it's hard for you to believe, but I'm not going to hurt you."

"But if I lie back, I can't see you," Glory complained mutinously, that full lower lip of hers formed into a beguiling pout. "And I want to see everything. Would you mind standing back a little?"

Bill stared at her, open-mouthed. "Mind? Of course, I don't mind," he managed, but as her eyes began their exploration of his body, further words failed him. Her intent gaze had an immediate and very obvious effect on him, but the sight of his urgent arousal didn't seem to frighten her in the least. Her eyes widened slightly, but they didn't move away, and suddenly, Bill felt as if he were the one who was burning up.

"You're so beautiful," Glory breathed in awe, then her lips curved in an impish grin. "And besides inciting some other enjoyable reactions, I can make *your* skin glow, too."

"Why you little—" Bill launched himself at the bed, covering her lips with his before her triumphant giggle could escape. He kissed her until they were both enflamed to the point of gasping, then lifted his head and gazed down at her with the most incredulous expression on his face. "I've never wanted anyone this much in my life."

"I want you, too," she whispered, lifting her hips obediently as he began pulling off her jeans, forgetting all of her previous worries. "It seems as though I've waited forever for this moment."

"That last night in Hubbard's Grove seems like another lifetime," he muttered darkly, reminding her that she knew very little about what he'd done since leaving town. For all she knew, over the past ten years he could have bedded down with entire hordes of eager women or maybe he'd wanted just one—the redhead who'd provided him with a freckle-faced son. Glory wanted to ask about her, but was wise enough to realize that this was neither the time nor place. Then, when she felt his warm hand slide down her body, his fingers searing the skin of her hips and stomach, her brain quit functioning rationally.

Feeling her stiffen as he ran his hand down her sleek flank, Bill murmured, "Relax, honey. There's nothing to be afraid of."

Even with that assurance, Glory flinched when he parted her legs with his thigh and he touched her in the place that had yet to know the feel of a man's caress. "Don't tense up," he whispered, but she found it impossible to follow that request as his gentle fingers stroked between the delicate silken folds. With each increasingly intimate caress, hot liquid sensation shot through her body, making her whimper.

Bill suppressed a groan, her throaty cries exciting him almost beyond bearing. He knew he was the first man to hear them, the first man to discover that Glory didn't know how to hold back. She arched her hips, her body trembling with the sweet need that he was creating in her, yet he didn't dare satisfy that primal craving until he learned if she could accommodate him without pain.

He felt the tremors begin when he probed gently inside her, not knowing how she was going to react to the final intimacy, but awed by the thought. She was incredibly responsive, and with every movement of her slender body, the demands of his intensified. Holding on to the last shreds of his sanity, he fumbled for the small packet on the mattress between them. He wanted to protect her, but found that there was no protection for himself when Glory's soft, warm fingers came to his aid. Once the feat was accomplished, Bill knew he couldn't wait a second longer.

He moved over her, every muscle in his body taut with the savage tension of restraint as he probed gently, waiting for her to cry out as he slowly thrust deeper. After a hellish eternity of keeping himself under control, he felt the resistance, but Glory's only response to its removal was a tiny gasp. At the small, relieved sound, his body surged forward, controlled by a power that went far beyond the physical.

As he increased the tempo of his thrusts, Glory felt a savage knot of pure pleasure coil within her. The tension drew tighter and tighter, until her body twisted and writhed for release. Her eyes flew open to find him gazing down at her startled face, and he smiled through his own torment because he was caught up in the same spiraling tension, and watching her pleasure increased the intensity of his own.

The spring of sensation snapped them both out of control at the same time, exploding around and within them, as they clung to each other, helplessly, joyously, shaking in the throes of utter fulfillment. Glory arched her neck, her fingers biting into Bill's shoulders, as the rippling shudders came, and as the first one hit, she cried out his name.

"Oh, Gloria!" Bill groaned as he felt her convulse around him, stunned by the heat of her passion and awed by the power she possessed in a body so small. To prevent himself from crushing her as he trembled on the edge of his own mind-shattering release, he rolled her on top of him, arching his hips as she claimed what should have been hers for almost a decade.

It was a long time before he found the strength to open his eyes, but he certainly liked what he saw when he did. Glory was still lying on top of him, her flaming hair spread out over his chest, her cheek resting over his heart and her slender legs entangled with his. He reached up and touched her hair, suddenly afraid that this was only another one of his dreams and that she was going to disappear as she always had before.

At the feel of his hand in her hair, Glory lifted her head, the adoration in her blue eyes better than any reaction he'd imagined in his fantasies. "I liked that," she murmured softly. "I liked it, a lot."

"Me, too," Bill replied, wondering if a bigger understatement had ever been spoken by a man.

"Wanna do it again?" she asked hopefully, nuzzling her face against his shoulder.

Bill could barely dredge up the energy to throw up his hands, his eyelids so heavy that he couldn't keep his eyes open. "After that marathon effort, it's all I can do just to breathe."

In mock indignation, Glory rolled off to one side and demanded, "Is making love with me such an effort?" but her question didn't receive a response, for Bill was already fast asleep, his body completely relaxed, his limbs sprawled out to the four corners of the rumpled sheets.

"Poor exhausted man," Glory crooned as she pulled the coverlet over them both and tucked her head beneath one outstretched arm, snuggling close to his side. "It finally caught up with you, didn't it?"

Glory went perfectly still as she heard Bill mumble something, but it didn't sound like an answer to her question. She thought he said something about not being alone anymore, but she was still puzzling over the possibilities when she drifted off to sleep herself.

Eight

———

Watching Bill sleep was an extremely enjoyable way to spend her time, Glory decided the next morning. Rolling over onto her stomach, she propped her head up on both hands, a blissful smile on her lips. Even so, after spending close to a half an hour indulging herself with the glorious sight of that devilishly handsome face in repose and all those beautifully naked muscles stretched out close beside her, she was definitely starting to think about an even more enjoyable pastime.

Unfortunately, although her insides were rapidly melting, Bill was completely oblivious to her fevered agitation. His lashes lay dark and heavy against his tanned cheeks, and his mouth was slightly parted as he breathed with a regularity that Glory hadn't been able to match for several, increasingly longer minutes.

A glance at the clock on her nightstand told her that he had slept for nearly ten hours. Considering the exhausted state he'd been in last night, Glory knew that he could probably do with even more rest, but the temptation to touch him was just too strong. Reaching out with one hand, she trailed her fingers along the soft, springy arrow of hair that angled across and down his wide chest, then lower to the warm, smooth silk of his lean hips and flat stomach. He felt so good to the touch, so very good.

"Oh, Billy," she breathed, leaning over him to brush her lips across the broad expanse of one bronzed shoulder. The man didn't stir by so much as a muscle, so her actions grew bolder. She nuzzled his throat with her lips, kissing the warm skin, but even when she nibbled his ear affectionately, Bill slept on.

Eventually, she gave up on her hopes for his active participation, but that didn't stop her from enjoying herself. Eyes closed in dreamy rapture, she adored his body with her hands, exploring him as she'd longed to do all these years. With every touch, the marvelous differences between male and female increased the desire building inside her. As her heart began beating more and more rapidly, she devoutly wished that the particular male beside her would wake up and appreciate her loving attentions, but nothing she tried seemed to have any kind of effect.

However, when she slid her fingers beneath the sheet draped loosely over his hips, she was astonished to discover that even in sleep, arousing him to the same state she was in wasn't going to present any difficulty for her whatsoever. Bill might not be actively aware of her wishes, but one part of him seemed more than willing to take up where they'd left off the previous night.

Since she felt as if there was a coiled spring inside her, drawing tighter and tighter with every breath she drew, Glory took wanton advantage of her discovery. She curled her hand around him, stroking gently. He throbbed beneath her caressing fingers and she felt an answering throb deep within herself, exciting her even more. As naked as he, she pressed herself closer to his side, absorbing his body heat, revelling in the knowledge that her touch could generate such a strong reaction.

"What the—!"

Bill's hand shot out to fasten over hers, trapping her palm against his burning flesh. Still groggy, he turned his head, trying to focus. "Glory?" he croaked hoarsely, blinking his eyes until he could fix her with a disbelieving stare. "Am I dreaming?"

Glory smiled at him, sensuously moving her fingers beneath his imprisoning hand. "Does this feel as if you are?"

Bill groaned as a shaft of pure white-hot pleasure shot through his loins, arching his back and clenching his thighs. Glory's hand slipped out from beneath his, but the pleasure continued. He felt the silky sweep of her hair across the sensitive skin of his bare stomach, and then she kissed him!

Suddenly, he was acutely aware that he was teetering on the very brink of ecstasy with only the beginnings of a notion as to how he'd arrived. "Glory!"

Hearing the urgency in his voice, Glory attempted to lift her body on top of his, but before she could move, Bill had her shoulders pinned to the mattress and his legs between hers. He possessed her lips with his—fierce and demanding, hungry and wild. And he possessed her body with equal hunger.

Glory gasped in delight at Bill's passionate intensity, amazed that the wonderful sensations he was inspiring with his hands and mouth were no less wonderful, yet so entirely different than what she'd felt with him the night before. This morning he wasn't being mindful of her inexperience or concerned about causing her pain. Tenderness had no part in their lovemaking. This time they came together as equals, in a fever of frenzy, giving everything and taking all with matching zeal.

Glory shivered and shuddered, digging her hands restlessly into his taut buttocks as Bill quickened his movements. His hair-roughened chest was an exquisite torment against her aching breasts, sensitizing her nipples to the point that every breath he drew made her whimper. His muscled body kept hers pinned to the bed, and she moaned in pleasure as she wrapped her legs around his hips, driving him more deeply inside her. "Now, Billy. Now!"

She heard his quick intake of breath, felt a reflexive clenching of his arms around her, and then he was slamming into her with primitive force and she was loving it. She clung to him, gasping, as the coil within her snapped and sent her spinning away, taking Bill with her.

It was a long, long time before either of them could summon the energy to speak, but Bill finally regained enough strength to lift his head away from her wondrously soft breasts. At the sight of Glory's sublime smile, he asked thickly, "Happy now?"

Glory remembered the sarcastic tone he'd used the last time he'd asked her that question and her smile widened. "Very happy," she murmured in satisfaction. Bill rolled onto his side and propped himself on one arm to gaze at her, his expression still slightly dazed. "You wanted me to take you like that?" he demanded in amazement. "Fast and hard with no preliminaries?"

"You slept through most of those, but *I* enjoyed them immensely," Glory informed him cheekily, her mouth falling open when she noticed the sudden rise of color in his face. "Why William Daniel McCann, you're actually blushing!"

He eyed her warily, as if he wasn't quite sure how to handle her anymore, which Glory found extremely gratifying. "I didn't expect to wake up to find you stroking my... and then you—" His voice broke off abruptly and beneath the shadowy stubble of his morning beard, Glory saw another slight rush of color.

Her delighted laughter made him scowl. "You're asking for it, woman," he growled, annoyed with his adolescent response to her teasing. It was just that he'd never felt so completely vulnerable before, and he was stunned by the power Glory wielded over him. He knew that she didn't have an unkind bone in her body, but being controlled to such an extent by any woman, even Glory, terrified him. "If you remember, *I'm* supposed to be the aggressor here. You're supposed to be the shy novice."

"Besides being a fast learner, a vivid imagination comes in very handy at times," Glory confided blithely. "And since I know that reality is infinitely more satisfying, I think you can forget about shy."

"Amazing," Bill said, but there was still a touch of censure in his voice.

Hearing it, Glory frowned in consternation. "I'm sorry."

"Sorry...sorry for what?"

"You don't like it when a woman makes the first move."

Bill was instantly contrite, appalled by the misinterpretation she'd put on his reactions to her seduction. She may have caught him off guard, but after the incredible pleasure she'd given him this morning, Glory had permission to put any moves on him she wanted, anytime, anyplace, anywhere.

"That depends on the woman," he informed her, but then was struck by an extremely unsettling thought. He'd never enjoyed making love so much in his life, but they'd come together without using any form of protection, an oversight that could easily have disastrous results. The violet color in his eyes changed to black as he remembered the kind of pain he'd brought upon himself the one other time he'd been negligent.

"And when that woman is me?" Glory whispered.

Hearing the anxiety in her voice, Bill wrenched his thoughts back to the present. Glory wasn't like that, he reminded himself. She wasn't, and even if she had been, he was a lot older and wiser now than he'd been at twenty-one. "Don't worry, sweetheart," he assured her. "Where you're concerned, I'll gladly hand over the lead. I thought I'd just made that embarrassingly obvious."

Tentatively, Glory asked, "So you liked it?"

"Liked it! The instant I felt your mouth on me, I was so wild to have you that I couldn't wait. It was only afterward that I realized you might not have been ready, and I didn't like that possibility at all. I'd like to think that I'm an unselfish lover, and up until a few minutes ago, I've never taken my own pleasure before finding out if my partner was fully satisfied."

In Bill's estimation, watching her response to his explanation was like watching the sun come out from behind a gray cloud. "Oh, I was ready," she stated throatily. "More than ready."

A second later, however, the clouds were back— very dark, stormy clouds that Bill couldn't have predicted unless he'd been aware of how often Glory had imagined him in the arms of some woman besides herself. Suddenly, she had to know just how many partners they were talking about. Ten? Twenty? Hundreds? Since he'd told her next to nothing about the years he'd been away, she had absolutely no way of knowing. "Just how generous are you with your lovemaking?"

"Are you asking me to show you how unselfish I can be in bed?"

Bill's conceited grin made Glory furious. "Of course not! I already know what an expert lover you are."

"Then what *are* you asking?"

Glory sat up and scooted backward on her bottom until she was leaning against the headboard. The abrupt action told Bill that she was in no mood for a repeat performance of their recent endeavors, and though he didn't understand her sudden need to talk, he sat up beside her.

Since they were both still naked, however, Glory wasn't that pleased by the change in their positions. Reaching down for the sheet, she pulled it over them both, her face flushing at Bill's knowing grin as she removed all further visual distractions. "I was asking if you've made love to hundreds of women or if I'm somewhat higher up on your list of conquests."

Thoroughly taken aback, Bill croaked, "Hundreds!"

His astonished reaction gladdened Glory's heart, but her need to know if he'd changed from the love-'em-and-leave-'em type he'd once been still wasn't satisfied. "You're a red-blooded bachelor in the prime of your life, and it's obvious that you like women and that women like you. As a teenager, you could've had any girl you wanted, and I imagine the same thing holds true today."

"I realize that Hillsborough isn't exactly the medical-news capital of the world," Bill stated mockingly, disliking heartily the direction this conversation was taking. "But surely even *you've* heard that indiscriminate bedhopping can be fatal."

His gaze drifted to the creamy tops of her breasts exposed above the sheet, his eyes gleaming wickedly. "Nowadays, a man has to be very choosy."

If he expected her to take that last comment as a compliment, he would just have to think again, Glory fumed. Still, she had too much pride to come right out and ask him to place a number on his past conquests. Neither was she about to drop the subject. He'd admitted to being an unselfish lover, and now that she knew exactly what kind of generosity he was talking about, she was frightened by the thought that she was only one woman among many.

Dwelling on that possibility not only frightened her, but filled her with a raging jealousy. Maybe it was only a coincidence, but she knew of at least two other women besides herself who'd benefited from his loving attentions and she also knew that both of them had shared her hair color, which made her wonder if she was really special to him or if Bill was just running true to his type.

"Okay," she conceded tightly, slapping his hand away when he attempted to wrap an errant curl of her hair around his finger. "In light of the current health risks, I can understand why you'd narrow your scope of choices. So does that mean you only have sex with virgins? Or is red hair another one of your requirements?"

"What?"

"If you recall, Nell Harper is a redhead, and of course, there's me, and I can also assume by Jamie's looks that his mother wasn't a classic blond or a brunette. So that's three, and—"

"Dammit, Glory! If you know what's good for you, you'll stop right there!" Bill exclaimed in growing outrage. "This conversation is becoming ridiculous."

"Even nowadays?" Glory inquired sarcastically, still smouldering over his mocking comment about Hillsborough's lack of sophistication when it came to matters of sex. "Speaking from a strictly medical standpoint, I believe I'd just earned the right to know a few things about your romantic history."

Bill glared at her, his temper warring with the utter disbelief that Glory, the woman who'd just loved him with all the passion in her sweet, innocent body, was actually talking to him like this. "Then for your information, I never had sex with Nell Harper."

Glory's disbelieving sniff was audible, and that made him really lose his temper. "What the hell kind of lowlife do you take me for, anyway? I only went out with the girl once and that was because she wouldn't take no for an answer!"

"That's not what *she* said," Glory informed him haughtily, but the rejoinder sounded childish and catty even to her own ears.

"I don't give a damn what that ninny said," Bill shot back angrily. "Nor do I like what you're implying, but just to keep the medical record straight, let me assure you that there's nothing wrong with me."

Sensing the genuine hurt behind that snarl, Glory retracted her claws, shamefully aware that she'd taken this line of questioning much too far. "I never thought there was."

"Then why the inquisition?"

Glory flushed guiltily. She knew that any good relationship had to be based on honesty, but she was too cowardly to come right out and ask if he'd ever been deeply in love with any of the other women he'd taken to bed, especially the woman who'd given him his son. Ever since he'd told her that he hadn't been married to Jamie's mother, she'd spent hours wondering about that relationship, but after that first day at the picnic, he'd never brought up the subject again.

"Glory?" Bill demanded in exasperation. "Will you kindly tell me what has prompted all this?"

With a small sigh of surrender, Glory admitted, "To tell you the truth, I'm feeling jealous."

"Of Nell Harper!"

"Of Jamie's mother."

Bill stared at her without speaking for several seconds, but his expression remained closed, shutting out Glory's fears and her unwelcome curiosity about that dark period in his life. When he felt ready to talk to her about Melanie Carstairs he would, but it certainly wasn't going to happen at this inopportune time, and certainly not when he and Glory were still in bed together. What the two of them had just shared was too good, too honest, and it made him sick to remember that he'd once settled for something far less with a woman who didn't know the meaning of the word *give*.

"Believe me. There's nothing for you to be jealous of," he bit out, reluctant to taint the air between them with the mention of Melanie's name, yet understanding Glory's need for reassurance. "I didn't love the woman and she didn't love me."

Gazing deeply into his dark eyes, all Glory could see was a black insurmountable wall he refused to allow her to climb. "'The *woman*'? You've had a child by her," she reminded him harshly. "Yet, you won't even tell me her name?"

"Melanie," Bill ground out harshly. "Her name was Melanie. Now are you satisfied?"

Glory searched his shuttered features once more, and her heart fell even further. She believed that he'd never been in love with this Melanie, but his disclosure didn't make her happy or even help to relieve her mind. She could sense the pain beneath his words, but also his reluctance to share it, and beyond that, his anger that she would expect him to. "If that's all you're willing to tell me, I guess I'll have to be satisfied."

"For the time being, that's all you need to know." Bill said, but to his frustration, Glory still refused to drop the matter.

"In other words, your personal life is none of my business."

"In other words, I don't want to talk about it right now," he replied in an aggrieved tone.

As devastating as it was for her to accept, Glory had just gotten the only answer that truly mattered. Bill was perfectly willing to share his body with her, but that's where it ended. He didn't need to put up a Keep Out sign for her to realize that she wasn't welcome in his innermost thoughts and feelings. That lonely young boy she'd befriended so long ago no longer needed anybody.

Arms folded across her chest, she muttered. "I guess that's it then."

"What's it?"

Somehow, Glory managed to get the necessary words out from between her cold, bloodless lips. "What we enjoyed last night and this morning didn't have anything to do with love. That being the case, whatever you choose to do with your life from now on is also none of my business."

"Dammit, Glory! Why in hell are you doing this to me?" Bill swore, reading her intention to leave the bed and preventing it by clamping his hand over her wrist. "Since I got back to town, this is the first weekend I've taken off. This time together is too valuable for us to spend it arguing. Now that we've rediscovered what we once had, nothing else that happened in the past should matter."

Lifting her hand to his mouth, he pressed a kiss in her palm. "This is all that matters."

Knowing that he honestly believed that, Glory tugged her arm out of his grasp. "Maybe sex is all that matters to you, but I need much more from a man," she exclaimed fiercely. "And just for the record, let me tell you another thing. That cold, impersonal attitude might work just fine with your employees, Big Bill McCann, but I don't work for you, and I won't allow you to place me on a need-to-know basis."

That said, she swung her legs over the side of the bed, dragging the sheet with her. Wrapping herself in as much dignity as was possible under these wretched circumstances, she walked out of the room, head held high as she marched down the hall. Before closing the door to the bathroom after herself, she stopped to look back.

"I think it would be best if you left now," she stated curtly, unable to hide the bitterness in her tone. "I imagine Jamie's wide awake by now and missing his daddy. Maybe you should spare *him* some of your valuable time."

Bill stared at the spot where she'd stood long after she'd disappeared inside the bathroom. It took a while for the pain she'd inflicted to work its way through his shock and confusion, but when it arrived, it took hold of him with a vengeance. He was willing to concede that he probably deserved that last verbal shot about Jamie, but he didn't deserve the other.

Big Bill McCann. That's what she'd called him, and that's how she thought of him, just because he wasn't prepared to spill his guts for her on demand. Big Bill McCann, indeed!

Rage was a very effective motivator and it brought Bill up from the bed with a vehement oath. He had thought she was different, but Glory had judged him just as all the other small-minded people in this town had. As far as she and everyone else was concerned, it didn't matter what he said or did, he would always be looked on as his father's son.

Stalking furiously around the room, he picked up his clothes but quickly lost his patience when he could only come up with one loafer. A few moments later, he left without it, feeling like an irate male Cinderella limping away from the ball. Once he was inside his car and racing up the mountainside, he managed to bring his anger under control, but he continued to identify with that fairy tale more than he cared to.

If it wasn't for Jamie, the one bright shiny spot in his future, he would be quite willing to race Cinderella for the nearest ash heap. He'd never put much faith in happy endings, and Glory had certainly proved that he was right to have his doubts. For a few brief shining moments, he'd actually entertained the notion that a beautiful fairy princess might be able to restore his lost faith in humanity, but trusting in that kind of magic was about as worthwhile as building castles in the sky.

Bill knew all about castles. He and Jamie lived in the biggest one around. "And this monstrosity sure as hell ain't Camelot!" Bill observed darkly. Unleashing the full horsepower beneath the hood of his shiny blue carriage, he sped through the heavy iron gates and careened to stop before the white marble balustrade that fronted his self-imposed prison.

As usual, Ida May dropped Jamie off at the day-care center by nine o'clock on Monday morning. Glory was angry with herself for being the least bit curious, but she found herself drawing him away from the game he was playing with the other children in order to ask about his weekend. "I know you were hoping your dad could take you fishing on Saturday, Jamie. Were you able to go?"

"Nope," Jamie replied, but surprisingly, the boy didn't sound that disappointed.

Praying that his uncaring tone didn't reflect the calm of resignation, Glory asked, "What did you do then?"

"Dad took me to a swamp full of green slime."

Glory bit her lip. She knew exactly what swamp Jamie was talking about, just as she knew that it had once been his father's only refuge. Did Bill still think of the place that way? Had she hurt him so badly that he'd gone there to lick his wounds, or had he returned to his childhood retreat for some other reason? "Did you have fun at the swamp?"

Jamie's expression grew pensive. "Well, the first thing Dad did was show me how to breathe through a slimy weed. He says he learned how from a real famous guy named Davey Crockett, but I still don't see why he thinks it's so fun."

"It wasn't fun for you?"

"It was kinda yucky," Jamie admitted, but then his features brightened. "But after we got done doing that we jumped in the swimming hole with no clothes on and caught some frogs. Dad even let me take the biggest one home with us. Ida May threw a fit when she saw it."

Glory's lips twitched. "I'll bet."

Jamie grinned at the memory. "But Dad said it was our house now and not some sacred maus— maseo—"

"Mausoleum?"

"Uh-huh," Jamie agreed with her pronunciation of the word, his eyes lit with enthusiasm as he added, "So that's why we can mess everything up and keep frogs in it if we want. And guess what else?"

"What?"

"I'm getting my very own dog, and Dad says it can sleep in my room with me! He says that when he was little, he used to get scared at night sometimes, too, and he always wished he had a dog." Frowning slightly, he continued, "I think if he was really scared bad, his mamma and daddy should'a got him a dog, even if it made messes in the house. Don't you?"

Glory managed to get her reply past the sudden lump in her throat. "Yes, I do."

Jamie nodded at her in approval. "Don't tell my dad, but when he gets me my dog, I'm gonna share him."

As if disclosing a solemn secret but knowing he could trust her to understand, he leaned closer to her and whispered. "My dad gets some real bad dreams and sometimes I think he's scared just like me."

Glory reached out to ruffle Jamie's hair, her eyes unnaturally bright. "Everyone gets scared sometimes and has bad dreams—even big, strong men."

"Dad says my dog's gonna chase my bad dreams away, so I'm gonna let him sleep in Dad's room sometimes, too. Besides, I think Dad needs my new dog worse than me."

"Why do you think that?"

"Cuz I'm making lots and lots of new friends, but he don't have nobody but me," Jamie replied, then, seeing that it was his turn to run around inside the circle of children, he scampered away from her to rejoin the game.

Deep in thought, Glory stared after him for several seconds before turning away, but Cindy Potter noticed her pained expression and followed her out into the hallway. "Is something worryin' ya', Glory?" she asked with concern.

Glory didn't hesitate to tell her. "Jamie McCann just said something to me that makes me wonder how things are going up at the mill since his father took over. I understand that he's making some pretty big changes. How does your Ben feel about them?"

Cindy shrugged. "Same as other folks, I imagine. Big Will was always promisin' that things would get better by and by, but all of us knew better than to believe him, and we ain't about to be believin' his son. We're drawin' our wages and all, but that's not worth braggin' about, and there's plenty of men still out of work."

"But if Bill does come through on his promises, they'll be called back eventually," Glory insisted. "And Kenny tells me that they've already landed one or two big contracts for the upcoming year."

"Well, we ain't seen the good of that yet," Cindy reminded her stubbornly. "And considerin' how a

McCann's still runnin' the place, who's to say we ever will?"

Glory didn't need to hear anymore to understand what kind of odds Bill was up against, and because she still loved him and would always love him, she felt compelled to reduce those odds. A few nights ago, Bill had more or less spelled out that he would either make a success of the business or die trying, and she believed him. No matter what the status of their personal relationship, she also believed that Bill and his young son had as much right to live in these beautiful mountains as anyone else. She remembered what her Aunt Ophelia had said on the Fourth of July, *That boy's place is here, and always has been.*

"I say so," Glory stated firmly. "William McCann is nothing like his father."

"S'pose that could be true, but he's still an outsider to be sure. Left town without looking back, till his rich daddy up and died. Like my Ben says, that man's been gone so long, he don't know or care how we do things in these parts."

"I'd say he cares very much about the welfare of this community," Glory retorted fiercely. "He could have sold McCann Lumber and made a substantial profit for himself, but he didn't do that, did he? If he really were the outsider everyone makes him out to be, the mill would be shut down for good by now and everybody would be out of work—permanently."

"Reckon that's so," Cindy conceded, her brow furrowing uncertainly.

Seeing that thoughtful look, Glory promptly applied more pressure. "I also understand that Bill is about to start a profit-sharing program that will give everyone a share in the eventual outcome of the business. Now I ask you, Cindy, would Big Will have even considered such a move?''

The young woman's eyes widened incredulously. ''Are you sayin' that this profit-sharing notion is truly going to happen?''

Glory didn't know that for sure, but she did know Bill. ''Indeed I am.''

''Well, you've always been as good as your word, Glory Hubbard, so it must be so,'' Cindy murmured excitedly, her eyes straying to the nearby wall phone. ''Just wait till folks hear about this.''

''Will you do me a favor?'' Glory asked, suppressing her gratified smile.

''Sure.''

''When the time comes, will you remind people that they didn't hear about profit sharing from me first? They heard it from Billy D. McCann.''

Nine

———

It was the end of another seemingly endless week, but for once, Bill had reason to smile. The personal side of his life might be at a new low, but at last things seemed to be looking up on the business end. Tossing the set of papers he'd just been given down on his desk, he reached across it to shake the hand of his top salesman. "Great job, Murphy," he complimented. "I didn't think Banner Construction was ever going to sign a contract with us, no matter what kind of deal we were willing to offer. Mind telling me how you managed it?"

Randolph Murphy gave a modest shrug, but his brown eyes were sparkling with triumph as he accepted Bill's hand. "Easy," he replied with a toothy grin that made him look far younger than his thirty-five years. "Royal Banner's been feudin' with Tom Dillon for more years than I can remember. I also happen to know that they're both vying for jobs in that new housing project being built over in Center City next year. When I told ol' Royal that Dillon Homes had put an order in with us two weeks ago for all the plywood and particle board we could process before spring, he assumed that Tom was hoping to get the jump on him.''

"So just to be on the safe side, he doubled Dillon's order,'' Bill concluded dryly.

"You got it,'' Randolph replied, grinning as he folded his long, lanky body into the chair in front of Bill's desk.

Bill returned the man's smile, then placed his hand over the big adding machine that took up entirely too much space on one side of his desk. After running a series of numbers through the antiquated instrument, he pulled down on the lever, his brows going up when he read the total. ''We're talking some pretty big numbers here, Murphy.''

"Huge,'' Randolph agreed.

"And far more overtime than I'm willing to pay.''

Randolph's face fell. ''Geez! You're going to back out on this sweet of a deal?''

Bill heard the wealth of disappointment behind the man's question, but none of the hostility he would've expected him to feel upon reaching such a conclusion. It might have been kinder of him to immediately relieve the man's mind, but suddenly Bill realized that Murphy wasn't the only one of his employees who'd undergone a dramatic change in attitude over the past several weeks. Not only had the men in sales readily agreed to a reduction in their commissions, but the first week in August, his line foreman, Ben Potter, had come into the office to tell him that until the business was turned around in the right direction, he and the rest of his crew had agreed to keep on working at the same low wages.

Now that he thought about it, Bill realized that lately, even the formidable Miss Peabody had begun to act as if he were the boss and not some obnoxious whippersnapper who was attempting to usurp her authority. Was it possible that his employees were actually starting to trust in him and his decisions? Had they finally realized that he was his own man, and not some crafty clone of his father?

Unfortunately, he didn't have time to dwell on that possibility since a very downcast-looking salesman was still waiting for a response to his question. "You can take that woebegone expression off your face, Murphy. The deal stands. All I was saying is that we won't make our budget or our future deadlines unless we hire on more full-timers."

"We won't?"

The incredulous look on the man's face was so comical that Bill was hardpressed not to laugh. "Not the way I see it. With two jobs of this size on line at the same time, it's going to be far cheaper to pay out regular wages than pay out that much overtime."

Bill took Murphy's raised eyebrows and rapidly bobbing head as a sign of his total agreement. "Well then, why don't you go find Ken Hubbard and outline our problem to him," he suggested. "First thing Monday morning, the three of us can sit down together and formulate a list of the people we'll need and how to proceed with the callbacks."

"Yes, sir! I'll get right on that, sir!" Randolph exclaimed, his lean face wreathed in smiles as he leaped
out of his chair and made for the door.

Bill held up his hand to stop the man before he left.
"And, Murphy, until we know exactly how many
people we're talking about, I think we'd better keep
this new development under our hats. We still haven't
reached the point where we can rehire everybody we've
laid off in the past and I don't want to raise any false
hopes out there."

"You bet," Randolph replied, and before Bill could
say another word, he was out the door.

As he watched the excited man traveling from desk
to desk, passing on the good news to their wide-eyed
occupants, Bill sat back with a wry shake of his head.
"Not a damned thing's kept secret around here," he
grumbled in resignation, looking down at the signed
contract on his desk, then glancing up again when he
got the uncomfortable feeling that he was being stared
at. His scowling visual search for the culprit or cul-
prits proved useless, but noting the wide grins on the
faces of every man and woman who occupied the front
office, Bill could feel his own face turning red.

"Damn those windows," he swore, vastly relieved
when he heard the phone ring. Grateful for any dis-
traction, he made a grab for it, swiveling around in his
chair until his back was turned away from his avid
audience. "Bill McCann here."

At first Ida May talked so fast that Bill couldn't
understand her, but eventually he got her to slow down
long enough for him to comprehend that she couldn't
locate Jamie. She'd kept him home from day care that
morning with a case of the sniffles, but since the

weather was so warm, she'd allowed him to take his new puppy outside to play. The last time she'd seen him, Jamie had been chasing the lively chocolate Labrador down the drive.

Upon further questioning, Bill ascertained that both boy and dog had been missing for several hours. "Calm down, Ida. We'll find him," he assured the tearful woman, but his hand was shaking as he hung up the phone.

Knowing his son's penchant for wandering off by himself, especially after that incident when he'd ended up clear down at Glory's place, Bill had made it his top priority to teach the boy how to get back to the house from every likely location on the mountain. Yet, despite all those precautions Jamie had been missing for several hours.

"Is something wrong, young Will?" Miss Peabody shouted after him as he strode swiftly past her desk, but he barely heard her, and he didn't stop to answer or reprimand her for reverting to that juvenile title he disliked so heartily. Perhaps it was that oversight or the worried look on his face that had the woman reaching for the phone before Bill had made it past the last desk in the row, and he was totally unaware of the flurry of activity going on behind him as he rushed out of the building.

Ten minutes later, he'd driven out of town and was speeding down the road at the base of McCann Mountain. To his amazement, however, when he made the turnoff onto the winding road that led up the steep side, there were two slower moving cars ahead of him. "What the hell!" he exclaimed in vexation, slamming on his brakes to prevent a collision.

He tried once or twice, but the road was too narrow and curvy for him to pass safely, so he honked angrily on his horn, hoping whoever these slowpokes were, they would take the hint and pull off to the side. They didn't. Instead of giving him more room, the drivers simply honked back as if in cheerful acknowledgement of his presence behind them.

Adding more fuel to his temper, the driver of the lead car even had the nerve to stick his arm out the window and deliver a jaunty wave. For several more seconds, Bill was so irate he didn't even question why there would be two other cars on the road leading up to his house, but then he glanced into the rearview mirror and saw that he was now the third vehicle in what appeared to be an ever-growing parade. The only explanation Bill could think of for this astonishing turn of events was that somehow or another, these people had found out that Jamie was lost and they were planning to join in the search, an explanation that was confirmed the instant he parked his car in front of the house and got out.

"The boys and I were out at the community center when the call came in about your boy, Bill, and we aim to find him right quick," Caleb Bonner declared as he pushed open the door of the lead car then stepped away from it to start directing traffic. "Pull in over by the garage, Billy Roy. Hey! Jimmy Lee, don't you be parking that rattletrap of your'n on this here nice grass. Hector, we'll be needing your lanterns if we're still searching once it gets dark, so best bring your van up here close to the house where we can get at 'em quick."

Bill stood there in open-mouthed amazement as a long line of pickup trucks and cars turned in through the iron gates, their drivers obediently following Mayor Bonner's barked orders. He was still looking on in bemusement when Glory jumped down from the back of a pickup and came over to take hold of his arm. "The sisters will be here directly," she informed him. "If you don't mind, they'll be getting things started in the kitchen. As I'm sure you've already guessed, Ida May is perfectly useless at times like this."

"Getting things started?" Bill repeated stupidly, allowing her to lead him toward the house.

"Lemonade until the sun goes down and coffee and sandwiches after that," Glory told him briskly, understanding his confusion but hoping he would realize that now wasn't the time for any lengthy discussions. The sun was already low in the sky and they didn't have a whole lot of hours left before it sank behind the mountain, casting the entire forest into darkness. Finding Jamie was going to be hard enough in the daylight.

"Until the sun goes down," Bill said, in a tone that made it obvious that he was still not quite following the program but did comprehend the difficulties of scouring a heavily wooded area in the dark.

Noting the fear in his eyes, Glory tacked on hastily, "Of course, chances are that with all of us searching for him, Jamie will be home long before then, but as Aunt Ophelia always says, it's best to be prepared."

Once they were inside the large front hall, she shooed him toward the staircase, but since he looked as if he didn't have the first idea of why it was necessary for him to mount the stairs, she prompted, "You'll be wanting to change out of those good clothes. I'll go speak to Ida, then meet you back here in a couple of minutes."

Bill was on the third step before he snapped out of his befuddled stupor. Turning around to face her, he threw up his hands and started back down the stairs. "Who told you—why are all of you—I don't understand why—"

Glory cut him off in midsentence, her tone as tart and disapproving as any he'd ever heard her use. "Jamie is one of our own now, and whether you want to believe it or not, so are you."

As she watched his dark eyes widen at her verbal chastisement, Glory felt a deep, heartwrenching sadness. The magnitude of Bill's amazement was proof that he was so used to operating completely on his own that he truly believed he'd become an island unto himself. Answerable to no one, mistrusting everyone but his young son, he'd fooled himself into thinking that he didn't need anyone else.

Having been raised by loving people who knew how to nourish a child, having grown up in a family that had provided unconditional acceptance and kind understanding, Glory had always understood what Bill had yet to learn. What the poet had written was so very true, no man was an island. Like it or not, even the self-sufficient William Daniel McCann II was a piece of the continent, a part of the main.

"As I told you once before, it's only fair that you can count on us, since all of us are counting on you," she admonished more gently, hoping he didn't sense the pity she felt for his lack of understanding. "That's the way it works with people who care about each other, Billy D. McCann. Now, we've got a job to do, so will you please get going!''

Bill stared at her for a long, speechless moment, then abruptly turned his back, but Glory saw the hint of moisture in his eyes before he bounded up the stairs, and she had to blink her own eyes several times to keep them from misting up, as well. ''That's the way it works, my love,'' she whispered, then pulled herself together and headed for the kitchen to assure Cousin Ida that more help was on the way.

Five hours later, she and Bill were slagging through the muck surrounding the peat bog, their throats raw and voices hoarse from shouting Jamie's name. Every so often, they could hear the distant calls of other search parties combing the mountain, but the black, starless sky was still void of any flare signaling success. After so many hours of fruitless searching, it was beginning to seem as if the small boy and his dog had simply dropped off the face of the earth.

With every glance she stole at Bill, Glory saw how close he was to panic, and since her own imagination was running wild with negative thoughts, she couldn't really blame him. A front of dark clouds had swept up over the mountain at sunset, followed by a severe thunderstorm that had blown away the cloying heat and humidity of the late August day, but which had also left behind a cold wind and a thick cold mist to dampen both the body and the spirit. Once the cloud-burst was over and the search resumed, every person on the mountain had been motivated to greater effort by the same haunting picture—a shivering, wet, terri-fied little boy, possibly sick or badly hurt, huddled up in the dark forest somewhere with his poor, bedraggled puppy.

Yet, even with that heartbreaking picture firmly in everyone's mind, Jamie McCann remained lost.

Standard operating procedure for the community during this kind of crisis was to search for two hours, then check back in at home base to compare notes with the other tracking parties and also take a well-deserved breather. Where his son was concerned, however, Bill wasn't prepared to be practical or follow the established rules. Even after he'd tripped over a sharp branch and severely gashed his right leg, he'd refused to go back to the house to have the wound bandaged, and since Glory was almost as worried about him at this point as she was about Jamie, she hadn't taken a break yet, either.

She was wet, cold and exhausted, but Bill was in far worse shape than she, his limp becoming more noticeable with every step. His teeth were clenched tightly together, his jaw so rigidly set that she knew his injured leg was paining him a great deal more than he let on. Even so, the last time she'd suggested that he take a short rest, he'd practically snapped her head off. As the hours passed, the man grew increasingly more lame, but even if he ended up crawling through the underbrush on his hands and knees, Glory knew that he wouldn't stop searching until Jamie was found.

As stubborn as he, Glory was determined to be there when he finally admitted he was only human, but when the murky light of dawn sifted through the shrouded mist of the pine forest, she found herself lagging several yards behind him. Eventually, when they began climbing up the slippery granite rocks surrounding the waterfall, she was forced to stop in order to catch her breath. "I'm sorry, Bill. I have to rest here for a few seconds," she called after him, and to her everlasting surprise he immediately stopped climbing and turned around to face her.

As soon as she saw the tears making a dirty trail through the caked mud on his cheeks, her own exhaustion fled and she ran across the space separating them. "Oh, Billy," she cried, throwing her arms around his waist and hugging him tightly to absorb the shudders that wracked his body.

"Please, don't do this to yourself...please," she begged, and began spouting promises she prayed to God that she would be able to keep. "I swear to you, no matter how long it takes, we're going to find him and he's going to be all right. Jamie's going to be fine. I just know he will."

"Oh, God, Glory," Bill groaned harshly, holding her as tightly as she was holding him. "I haven't been this terrified since the day he was born. Where the hell is he? We've been searching all night. Why haven't we found him?"

"We will," Glory insisted, staggering beneath the unexpected pressure of his full weight as his leg buckled beneath him. It took a few moments for her to regain her balance, but she was finally able to serve as his crutch while he hobbled a few steps across the rocky terrain. "We have to get you back to base and have that leg looked at."

"I don't give a damn about my leg. I don't give a damn about anything but finding my son!"

After easing him down so he could sit on a flat ledge of rock, Glory sat down next to him, dashing her own tears off her cheeks with the back of her hand. "With so many people searching, it's only a matter of time."

The defeat in his tone made it clear that Bill didn't share her confidence. "Time doesn't matter if he's already dead."

Another deep shudder ripped through him, his breathing tortured as he cried out in anger and pain, "Oh, God! After all I went through just to see him safely born, I can't lose him now."

Glory took hold of both his hands and squeezed tightly, attempting to convey some sort of comfort, but instead of soothing him, her sympathetic action prompted him to keep talking. Dark eyes bleak with despair, he began the story he had never been willing to share before, not even with her. "I knew that getting myself hooked up with Melanie was probably a mistake, but I was very lonely and she made sure I knew how very available she was. At the time, I was working twelve-hour shifts on a highway construction crew in Oklahoma and she was a waitress in the local diner. I don't really remember how it actually happened, but one night, we ended up in bed together...."

Bill hesitated, as if highly uncomfortable, but then he cleared his throat and forced himself to continue. "Let's just say it wasn't the best experience for either one of us, and afterward, we both went our separate ways."

"Only Melanie got pregnant," Glory concluded sadly.

Bill nodded. "I hadn't seen her for several months, and by the time she chose to tell me, it was already too late for an abortion. But then, that was part of her grand plan.''

Glory frowned, wanting to ask him what plan he was talking about, but the look on his face warned her not to interrupt. ''Like the gallant young fool I was back then, I offered to do the honorable thing and marry her, but as it turned out, she wanted no part of that idea because she was already married.''

Bill nodded at Glory's incredulous expression. ''Legally, yes, but she told me that she'd left her husband months before meeting me.''

''And you believed her?''

''To be honest, I didn't know what to believe, but the timing was certainly right, and she swore that the baby was mine.''

''So you felt responsible,'' Glory guessed correctly.

''Just as she figured I would,'' Bill admitted self-derisively. ''And once I admitted that, she moved in for the kill.''

Upon making that chilling statement, he stopped talking, and Glory got the strong impression that he regretted telling her as much as he already had. To prevent him from leaving her with only half of the story, she encouraged him with what she considered to be the next logical conclusion. ''So, even though Melanie didn't expect you to marry her, she did expect you to support her financially throughout the remaining months of her pregnancy.''

''Not her as much as her drug habit,'' Bill bit out savagely. ''Which, along with her marriage, was another thing she'd neglected to reveal about herself. As far as being on the pill, she out-and-out lied to me about that. Three months after the fact, I came to find out that she'd deliberately set out to get pregnant."

"Why on earth would she want to do that!"

"For the very purpose of hitting me up for money at some later date. I thought she'd left her job at the diner voluntarily, since she seemed as uncomfortable around me as I was around her, but that wasn't how it happened. She got caught doing drugs for the second time and was fired. I guess that getting pregnant and appealing to me for financial support seemed a much better bet to her than trying to hold down another steady job."

"Oh, Lord," Glory whispered, appalled that any woman could be selfish enough to even contemplate doing such a thing.

"Naturally, as soon as I realized what bad shape she was in, I pleaded with her not to take any drugs, to give our baby a chance at life even if she didn't care about her own anymore, but she wouldn't listen. Melanie had me exactly where she wanted me. I was willing to do anything to keep her from destroying herself and my child at the same time, but no matter what I did, she always found some way to thwart me."

"How horrible," Glory murmured, imagining the kind of terror and helplessness he must have felt. "The woman was sick, Billy. Terribly, terribly sick."

"Sometimes I had a hard time believing that," he stated softly. "And that explanation didn't make what she was doing to me and my child any easier to accept."

"I'm sure it didn't," Glory agreed, but then she saw how wide the bloodstain on his leg had spread since they'd sat down, and her concern was promptly refocused on another area. "Before you say another word, I think I'd better take a look at that leg. You've lost too much blood for that to be just a shallow cut."

"The leg's fine," Bill said, glancing down unfeelingly at the long, jagged rip in his jeans. He could feel the blood running down his leg, pooling inside the sole of his boot, but he couldn't dredge up the will to do much about it. His entire body felt cold and numb, unable to function, except for that one overactive section of his brain that kept reeling with his earliest memories of Jamie and the woman who'd given birth to him—reeling around and around in his head like a bad movie that would never be over unless he finished his narration.

"Melanie seemed to take a perverse pleasure in the knowledge that she had the power to control someone else's behavior, since her addiction made it impossible for her to control herself. After putting us both through six months of pure unadulterated hell, she went into labor and died on the delivery table. I thought then that the worst of it was over. I was wrong."

"Jamie was born addicted," Glory murmured wretchedly, uncertain if she could bear listening to any more of this horror story without breaking down herself.

"Yes," Bill confirmed, his voice thick with a well-remembered grief. "I spent weeks sitting next to his incubator in the intensive-care unit, watching that incredibly tiny body struggling to overcome his addiction. Eventually, they allowed me to hold him, to comfort him through the shivers and shakes, all the while fearing that even if by some miracle he did manage to survive such agony, he'd be so severely retarded that he'd never lead a normal life."

"But Jamie *did* survive," Glory reminded, willing him to look on the positive side. "He may still be somewhat small for his age, but he's one of the brightest children I know."

"Odds were that he wouldn't be. At first the doctors didn't give him much chance of making it through his first year," Bill said. "Which was probably why the authorities made it so easy for me to take him home."

"Heaven help them if they hadn't!" Glory exclaimed, thoroughly outraged by the very idea that after all he'd gone through for his son, he might not have been allowed to claim Jamie as his own.

Bill tried to smile at her vehemence, but he couldn't. Now that he'd completed the story, his brain felt all woozy and he couldn't seem to find the strength to stand up. "I can't lose him, now, Glory," he murmured weakly. "I think it would kill me."

Glory gasped as Bill slumped over on top of her, for one instant thinking that his dire prediction was coming true, but then she realized that he'd fainted. In the time it took her to slip out from under the weight of his unconscious body and lie him down atop the wide ledge, his eyelids were already fluttering back open. "What happened?" he asked, attempting to lift his head, then discovering that he was still too light-headed to manage. Of course, that didn't stop him from trying again.

"You fainted," Glory told him, keeping one hand firmly planted in the center of his chest while she used the other to pull the belt out of her jeans.

"I didn't faint. I just had a dizzy spell," Bill disagreed, closing his fingers around her wrist in order to dislodge her hand. The fact that he couldn't manage it made him angry. "Come on, Glory. Let me the hell up! I've got to keep looking for Jamie."

"You, my friend, are not going anywhere," Glory retorted, but just so he could prove his incapacity to his mule-headed self, she removed her hand.

On his third attempt, Bill made it into a sitting position, but the movement nauseated him so badly that he lay right back down. "Damn it!"

While he struggled to keep from being sick, Glory ripped the tear in his jeans open farther. "No wonder you're weak!"

Upon closer examination, she saw that the five-inch gash angling upward from his knee was deep and oozing blood, but it was the puncture wound at the end of the cut that was his major problem. She could tell that he hadn't nicked the artery, but the free-flow of blood was enough to indicate that a large vein was involved. She made a tourniquet out of her belt and wrapped it around his thigh, nodding in satisfaction when the flow of blood slowed down considerably. "There, that ought to hold you until I can bring back some help."

As expected, Bill didn't cotton to that notion one bit. "If you expect me to lie here doing nothing when my boy is still out there someplace, you can forget it."

"What I expect you to do for once in your life is admit that you can't do it all alone," Glory retorted, stamping one foot in exasperation. "Bleeding to death because you're too all-fired stubborn to get your leg stitched up won't do Jamie a speck of good, and if you weren't so blasted egotistical, you'd realize that there are fifty other men out there who are far more capable of finding that boy than you are!''

"My ego has nothing to do with it," Bill snarled back. "In case you've forgotten, I grew up on this mountain and I know every inch of it like the back of my hand."

"In case *you've* forgotten, I grew up near here, too, and so did my brothers, and Caleb Potter and a half dozen other people!''

"But I'm Jamie's father!''

"So what?" Glory demanded, losing her temper and shouting, "I happen to love that little boy every bit as much as you!''

For once in his sorry life, Bill couldn't seem to manage a snappy comeback and Glory took swift advantage of the fact. "And if you still haven't figured out what all those other people are doing here, let me tell you. You and your son might not be true blood relation, but you're still considered kinfolk, and in this community, when trouble strikes, people support their kin!''

"Glory, it's not that I don't appreciate—'' Bill sat straight up, holding his head with one hand and pointing to the sky with the other. "Look up there!''

Glory followed the direction of his hand, spotted the signal flare that lit up the sky, then shot him a quelling look. "Imagine that," she declared smugly. "Somebody other than his pig-headed daddy just found Jamie.''

Ten

Bill took a sip of the strong, rich coffee Aunt Carrie had served to him, then with a contented sigh, leaned back against the fluffy pillows that Aunt Winnie had placed behind his back. He felt only a slight twinge of pain as he shifted his injured leg more comfortably on the white, upholstered ottoman that Aunt Ophelia had positioned in front of the low-slung leather couch. No matter what Glory thought, he didn't think he was going to need the pain pills Doc Sumner had left behind after cleansing his wound and stitching him up. True, he still felt a bit woozy from loss of blood, but the sight of Jamie frisking around with his puppy on the living room carpet was doing more to aid his recovery than any prescribed medicine.

It was obvious that Jamie, unlike his father, had suffered no visible ill effects from his long night on the mountain. After a nice hot bath and a big breakfast, the irrepressible six-year-old was up and at 'em again, not even exhibiting any sign of the sniffles he'd displayed before his ordeal had begun. Of course, chasing Cubby inside a hollow log and getting himself good and stuck had been a frightening experience for the boy, especially once it had gotten dark, but at least being inside the log had protected him and his pet from the cold wind and the rain. Those searching for him hadn't been so fortunate.

As Mayor Bonner kept repeating to anyone who cared to listen, "Neither he nor that little mut of his had a mark on 'em, whilst me and my boys'll be picking nettles out of our poor hides from here to Sunday. Had so much muck on our faces and duds, turns out that the young'n was more sceered of us than he was of stayin' trapped. Had to convince him we weren't a creepy gang of spooks before he'd let us get near enough to work him loose from that knotty hole."

Bill grinned as he watched Caleb collar a new arrival who'd been called to the house to deliver more bread and eggs. Considering the mayor's enthusiasm for retelling the tale, Bill figured that the daring rescue of Jamie McCann was going to be a hot topic of conversation down at the feed store. That is unless every citizen of Hillsborough planned to check in on the mountain this morning, which at the rate they'd been arriving, was entirely possible.

Rather than being annoyed by this invasion of what looked to be the entire populace of Jessup County, however, Bill was glad to see that once they got over their initial nervousness, these people felt welcome in his home. Considering the way they'd come to his aid yesterday, he was pleased to have them. If he lived to be a hundred, he would never forget the parade of people, many of them total strangers, who'd volunteered to help in the search for his missing son.

As Glory had taken great pleasure in reminding him, during times of crisis, the citizens of Hillsborough pulled together like kinfolk, and Bill was honored to think that this kinship now included both him and Jamie. He'd never felt this sense of belonging before, certainly not while his parents had been alive. But then, Big Will and Lorraine McCann had opened neither their hearts nor their elegant home to anyone who wasn't considered their social equal.

Gazing at the number of happy young children crawling around with Jamie on his mother's once-spotless white carpeting, Bill's smile grew wider. He might have been raised to think that possessions were worth more than people, especially children, but his son would grow up in a household where his friends were always welcome. As he listened to the pleasant hum of conversation and the sounds of laughter emanating from the kitchen and dining room, watched his neighbors crowding around the breakfast buffet that had been set out on the antique Louis XIV mahogany table, he felt his chest expanding with pleasure.

A man's home was his castle, but that castle didn't need to be a lonely and lifeless prison built to keep people out. If he'd learned anything since coming back home, especially during the past twenty-four hours, it was that he'd been responsible for his own isolation. Just because his parents had segregated themselves from others didn't mean that he had to erect the same impregnable walls. That was the lesson Glory had been trying to teach him ever since they'd been children, but until he'd witnessed the generosity of all those people combing the woods for his son, he hadn't understood what she'd been attempting to teach him.

Out of the corner of one eye, Bill caught a glimpse of shiny auburn hair and he turned his head to watch as Glory shouldered her way through the crowd surrounding the buffet. After setting a heaping tray of hot baking-powder biscuits on the center of the table, she picked up a coffeepot and began refilling empty cups. As if she hadn't spent a long, grueling night traipsing up and down the mountain after him, she accompanied every refill with a cheery word and a perky smile.

Catering to a group of this size was hard work, and even from his place in the living room, Bill could see the sheen of perspiration on her forehead. He also noticed the bit of dried leaves in her hair and that she was wearing the same checkered blouse and muddy jeans that she'd worn all night. Apparently, while he'd luxuriated in a long, hot shower, then outfitted himself in a set of clean, dry clothes, Glory being Glory, had settled for a quick lick and a promise, then joined the vast female army on duty downstairs.

Her cheeks were flushed from the heat of the kitchen, several short strands of hair were stuck to her hot skin, and her face was entirely devoid of makeup, but to Bill, no woman had ever looked more beautiful. However, upon noticing the dark violet shadows under her eyes and the tired stoop to her slender shoulders, he also decided that she was the most stub-

born and infuriating female he'd ever run across in his
life. As long as he'd known her, Gloria Eloise Hubbard had never been heard to cry uncle, but if she
didn't know when enough was enough, the man who
loved her certainly did.

Ever since he'd been carried upstairs to his bedroom on a stretcher, Bill had been treated like ailing
royalty, and under the circumstances, he wasn't above
taking some unfair advantage of his exalted position.
Unfortunately, he wasn't as able as he would have
liked to follow through on his grand plan, so as soon
as Ida May passed through the living room on her way
to the front door, he beckoned for her to approach his
throne and to do his regal bidding.

When he heard Glory's indignant shout, he'd only
limped as far as the bottom of the staircase. A second
later, Zeke Hubbard pushed open the kitchen door
and Bill saw a very red-faced cook being hoisted over
her oldest brother's shoulder. "Kenneth Hubbard!
You big lummox! Put me down this instant! Do you
hear?"

Of course, Glory's outcry drew a large, curious
crowd into the front hall, and when Zeke tried to
appease her with the announcement that Ken was only
following the boss's orders, all eyes turned to Bill.
Beginning to regret his high-handed tactics, Bill stammered what he hoped sounded like a plausible explanation, "Uhh...well...Glory's been working much
too hard today, but she's so blamed stubborn...eh,
what I mean is...well...I just thought it was about
time she...eh...took a load off her feet."

The lady in question lifted her head and shot him a
furious glare, but since Bill was standing too far out

of reach, she gave a more convenient target a sharp slap on the rump. Bill winced as Ken yelped, more and more convinced that he should've thought up some other way to make Glory see sense. One glance into her blue eyes told him that he was in very deep trouble for embarrassing her this way.

Bill cleared his throat, extremely embarrassed himself. He'd certainly never intended to cause such a scene, but there was nothing he could do about that now. Unfortunately, the whole damned countryside was witness to the fact that where Gloria Hubbard was concerned, he felt well within his rights to have her carried off, whether or not she went willingly.

Adding to his discomfort was the knowledge that in a small town like Hillsborough, such outrageous behavior was considered a public declaration of intent, and the fact that his accomplices were two of the woman's own brothers added even more credence to that possibility. Glory's reaction to being placed in such a position really worried him, especially when her Aunt Ophelia stepped forward to underscore his understanding of the situation.

"I say it's past time some man took her in hand, William McCann," the woman declared tartly, then waved one arm at her nephew. "You heard the man, Kenneth, now get along upstairs."

Suddenly quite glad that her humiliating position prevented anyone from seeing the fiery blush on her face, Glory cried, "Aunt Ophelia!"

Bill didn't know who was more astounded by the elderly woman's words, him, Glory or those watching the show, but they were soon to learn that the three sisters were all of the same mind. "I 'spect that you could use a bit of rest yourself, what with that leg painin' ya' so," Aunt Carrie decreed firmly, blue eyes twinkling with suppressed laughter as Kenneth struggled up the stairs with his kicking burden.

"And don't you be worryin' about how the rest of us down here are faring," she continued. "Most of these folks have already eaten their fill, and they'll be taking themselves off directly."

Aunt Winnie was just as quick to lend her assistance to the romantic cause. "Once they go, we'll do up these dishes and set things to rights, then be off ourselves so you two can have some peace. Ida's comin' into town with us, and don't you be worryin' none about Jamie. Liliah's invited him down to her house to play with her young'ns. Haven't you, dear?"

Right on cue, Kenny's wife piped in. "That's right. And, Bill, if we get back too late from the Center City fair, Jamie's more'n welcome to spend the night with us."

That amazing announcement raised several eyebrows, including Bill's, but Ida May was the only one to question the propriety of such an arrangement. In a whisper loud enough to wake the dead, she inquired of Winnifred, "Are you actually condoning these scandalous doings, Winnie Hubbard?"

"Indeed I am, and there's nothing scandalous about a man courtin' the woman he loves, Ida May Potter," Winnie whispered back and then suggested in a much louder tone, "David, Zeke, would you kindly help Bill. We wouldn't want him faintin' half way up those stairs."

"Yes, ma'am," the burly young men replied in unison, and before Bill could open his mouth to protest, his arms were draped over their broad shoulders. Then, showing him no more mercy than their older brother had shown their sister, they each took hold of a leg and lifted him off his feet. This demonstration of strength was greeted by loud applause and several admiring whistles.

In embarrassed silence, Bill suffered being carried up the stairs, sheepishly aware of how Glory must have felt when she'd been subjected to the same treatment. "Thanks, boys. I can make it from here," he informed them through gritted teeth once they reached the top landing, but he needn't have bothered. Even when he stopped trying to be polite, they still didn't put him down, but carried him the full length of the hall and into his bedroom, where a much smaller, but highly appreciative audience was waiting.

"Right over there boys," Ken directed helpfully, pointing at a spot on the king-size bed.

As he was dumped none too gently on the hard mattress, Bill couldn't bite back his pained grunt and Glory emitted what he thought was a most unkind giggle. "What's sauce for the goose, is sauce—"

"Oh, shut up," Bill growled at her, but she was still too vexed with him to be the least bit intimidated, and she knew just what to say to get a little of her own back.

"I realize that you consider yourself king of the mountain, but you can't just snap your fingers and have your lackeys cart me off to your royal chambers. That kind of uncivilized behavior might have worked in the dark ages, but this is the twentieth century, buster, and I've got something to say about who I have sex with."

Bill covered his eyes with one hand and groaned, "Geez, Glory! I know you're not very happy with me at the moment, but will you kindly give me a break? All three of your brothers have at least fifty pounds on me."

According to their amused expressions, Glory felt it was safe to assume that her disloyal siblings didn't feel the least bit compelled to defend her supposedly besmirched honor. "But we already know whose side these traitors are on, don't we?" she observed snidely, but Zeke was the only one who had the grace to look even slightly chagrined.

"Don't worry, Glory," he assured. "The sisters already took care of any nasty talk that might arise from this occasion."

Knowing that her aunts thought Bill McCann was the perfect man for her, Glory wasn't at all surprised by this information, and it was also true that she loved the man to death, but that didn't mean she was ready to let him off the hook so soon. "They actually approve of this high-handed rogue?"

"Seems like it," David said, as if he couldn't quite believe it himself. "But then, those romantic old souls have always taken kindly to McCann and his swaggerin' habits. Why, they still go on about that day you knocked him off his motorcycle and he ran you to ground like a hound after a vixen."

"Even I had to feel some admiration for him that day," Zeke admitted. "Glory sure 'nuff asked for what she got."

"When he's not making a public spectacle of himself, he's a real tribute to our sex," Ken agreed.

"Will you guys knock it off," Bill growled as the three grinning goons stood back from the bed and saluted smartly, but upon seeing that their respectful gesture had provoked a violent scowl, they made an extremely hasty retreat. Bill shook an exasperated fist at the closed door, recalling Glory's description of her siblings and agreeing with it. "Mean-minded turkeys!"

"Takes one to know one," Glory commented sweetly, but she swiftly changed her mocking tune when Bill glanced over at her with deliberate intent. "Now, now," she admonished, scooting back hastily on the mattress. "You started this, Billy D. McCann!"

"And now," he replied menacingly, "I'm going to finish it."

Glory rolled to one side, but even injured, Bill was much too quick for her. He managed to wrap one arm around her waist before she scrambled off the bed, but she resisted being dragged back against him and warned, "You'd better let go of me or you'll put too much strain on your bad leg."

"Gloria, you're so puny, the only strain you cause is to my temper," Bill retorted, then rolled over onto his side and tucked her underneath his outstretched body as if she weighed nothing. After kissing her breathless, he lifted his mouth in order to regain his own breath. "I'd better revise that. You also have a distinct talent for straining something else."

Glory wiggled her eyebrows at him, which made him scowl down at her ferociously. "Proud of that, are you?"

"Very proud," she agreed impishly, but to her surprise, Bill's expression didn't soften. "Do you feel threatened by that?"

"I feel threatened by everything you're capable of doing to me," he conceded reluctantly, bringing up one arm and tenderly brushing the back of his hand down her cheek. "To be honest, being this much in love with you scares me to death."

Glory's tone was assured. "But you're a very brave man, and your fondness for taking risks far outweighs your fear."

Bill gazed down at her incredulously for a few seconds, then shifted himself to one side and sat up. Glory gasped when she attempted to sit up beside him and he pushed her shoulders back down on the bed, but amazement was her next reaction as he reached down and began frisking her. "What on earth are you doing?" she demanded as he dug his fingers into the front pocket of her blouse, then began a diligent search of the back pockets of her jeans.

"Looking for those rose-colored glasses," he replied, running his hands down her legs. "You keep telling me that you've gotten rid of them, but after that last idiotic comment, I know they must be here somewhere."

"What *are* you talking about?" she inquired in confusion. "What idiotic comment?"

Bill reached down for her wrists then pulled her up so that they were facing each other, eye to eye. "*I'm* not the brave one here, Glory, and I'm not the one who enjoys taking risks. You are."

"Me!"

Bill nodded his head. "If you think back, I didn't venture into your secret hiding place. You stripped off all your clothes and jumped into mine, then challenged me to come join you."

"I was practically a baby," Glory complained indignantly. "You make it sound as if I was some kind of seductive siren."

"A tiny temptress even back then," Bill agreed. "But that was only the beginning of my downfall. After showing me how children are supposed to play, you dragged me back home with you, then browbeat your big brothers into being nice to me when what they probably wanted to do was take me down several well-deserved pegs."

Glory sniffed disdainfully. "They were all bigger than you. All I did was remind them that it wasn't very brave to pick on somebody who wasn't their own size."

"You were the smallest one of us all, but that didn't stop you from taking all three of them to task for my sake."

"I wouldn't call that bravery," Glory disagreed. "They're my brothers. I knew that they'd never hurt me."

Bill shook his head. "They never lifted a hand to you because they were afraid of what you'd do to them if they dared to try."

Glory looked stunned for a second, then she laughed. "Now that you mention it, when I truly care about something, I do have the tendency to rile up something awful. One time Zeke tipped a bird's nest out of a tree and I almost pulled every hair out of his head."

"Exactly," Bill confirmed smugly. "And even though I rile you greatly on occasion, you've never hidden the fact that you love me. Don't you know what kind of guts it takes to risk your heart like that? Wear your emotions on your sleeve for the whole world to see? Even back when we were teenagers, all you had to do was look at me and I knew exactly what you were feeling."

Glory shrugged, unable to accept his supposition that loving someone was an act of bravery. Of course, finding out that her great love for him hadn't been returned had hurt something awful, but even after suffering that kind of pain, she hadn't been able to stop caring. "It's not very nice of you to remind me that my feelings for you were so painfully obvious," she complained. "At the time, I thought I was acting very mature and sophisticated."

"If you're talking about that last night in Hunter's Grove, I agree," Bill allowed, finally able to smile at the memory. "You looked so damned beautiful, standing there in the moonlight in your new white dress, and I wanted you so badly. Turning around and walking away from you practically killed me, but if I'd made love to you that night, you would've ended up hating me."

"Never!" Glory burst out, but then Bill told her what his father had threatened to do to her brothers if he hadn't broken off their relationship, and she finally understood what had happened that night. "You did love me!"

"Very much," he murmured. "So much, that I couldn't stand being anywhere near you. After telling

Big Will what I thought of a man who would blackmail his own son, I left town."

His tone was so regretful that Glory flung her arms around his neck and kissed him full on the mouth. "I should've known it was something like that," she whispered, nuzzling his throat with her lips. "And I'm so sorry for doubting you."

"I've given you ample reason to doubt me," Bill reminded her gruffly, grasping her by the shoulders and setting her away from him before he gave into the temptation to postpone all that needed to be said and succumb to the need her lips were creating. "Both then and now, but I do love you. I've loved you since the very beginning."

"I know," Glory declared happily, a definite note of satisfaction in her tone as she added, "and after what you pulled just now, everyone else in town knows it, too."

"I don't care who knows it," Bill retorted, but then his expression became serious. "I hope you don't mind if we invite all of them to our wedding."

Glory wrinkled her nose in mock disgust. "As proposals go, Billy D. McCann, that one wasn't the most romantic, but since I'm already hopelessly compromised, I guess it'll have to do."

Bill's expression was so abashed that Glory laughed. "Don't look like that, you silly man. I'm just funnin' you."

Bill still felt the need to apologize. "I didn't mean for it to happen this way, Glory. I saw how tired you were and I knew you wouldn't take a rest unless I forced the issue."

"You did that all right."

"If I'd had it my way, I would've forced the issue ten years ago," Bill said. "And because Big Will made it impossible for me to have you, I left town a very angry young man. I hated him for denying me the only thing I needed to be happy, and to pay him back I was determined to remain outside his sphere of influence."

With a self-derisive shake of his head, he continued, "I learned pretty quickly that the world outside of Hillsborough could be just as rough. I cut myself out of my father's life, but at the same time, I cut myself off from everything I'd ever cared about. After a while, not caring about anyone or anything became a way of life with me...until Jamie."

Glory smiled compassionately. "Until Jamie."

Bill smiled back. "I wasn't aware of it at the time, but besides getting to know you again, he's the main reason I decided to stay on here and run the business. All those years I spent roaming aimlessly around, I'd tried to convince myself that roots weren't important. It was me and Jamie against the world, until we came back here and I realized that he needed so much more than I'd been giving him."

Glory took hold of his hand. "Don't be so hard on yourself," she scolded. "Jamie's always had what really counts, a father who loves him."

"But no place to call home," Bill reminded her. "No family other than me...no roots. I didn't have the right to deprive him of those things just because I'd been deprived."

"Jamie certainly doesn't strike me as a deprived child," Glory declared forthrightly. "He's wonderfully sensitive, wise beyond his years and he's got enough self-confidence for six children.''

Bill grinned at that. "Cocky. Just like his old man."

"Already developing the notorious McCann swagger," Glory agreed. "Which must be why all we Hubbard women simply adore him. I'm afraid that by the time he's sixteen, we'll have to beat the girls off him with a stick."

"Maybe he'll be lucky enough to find one brave enough to push him off his high horse whenever he needs it," Bill retorted dryly, leaning over to press a quick kiss on Glory's lips. "A pushy little woman like you."

"Now strikes me as the perfect time," Glory declared wrathfully, lifting her hands and twisting around so quickly that Bill was laying flat on his back before he knew what hit him.

He was about to utter a halfhearted protest, but his mouth was immediately smothered by a pair of soft lips, and Bill gave himself up to the exquisite pleasure. He enjoyed her sensual assault for several more minutes until the pain in his leg became so bad that he couldn't continue ignoring it. As usual, Glory was one step ahead of him, and by the time he managed to sit back up, she was on her way to the bathroom. "You'd best find yourself a more comfortable position for that leg, Billy D. McCann, because I'll be back right quick."

Bill contemplated her provocative warning for several moments, then thought better of taking it. He could hear the water running in the bathroom, and the image of Glory standing naked under his shower inspired too many pleasant memories for him to remain idle. The master bath boasted a huge, black marble tub, and with all those hanging ferns and potted plants situated around it, a man could easily compare it to that other pretty pool he'd spent so much time in as a kid. Even better, the blue-eyed nymph he would be sharing it with was no longer a child, and since he wasn't, either, Bill could think of lots of things they could do in the water besides swim.

In a matter of seconds, he'd stripped off his clothes. As he silently entered the bathroom, his eyes went to the gauzy shower curtain, happy to see that after turning on the shower, Glory hadn't bothered to open the drain. There were already several inches of water in the bottom of the tub, and once he turned on the four other spigots, the water would rise that much faster.

Glory was facing the front wall, so she didn't notice the tanned arm reaching inside the enclosure to turn a few knobs, but then Bill yanked back the curtain and stepped over the side of the tub. "I know this is rightly your own special place, Glory Hubbard, but I didn't figure you'd mind sharing it with a friend."

It took her a second to recover her shock, but then Glory laughed and it was the same joyful sound he'd heard the first day they'd met. Hands on her hips, she scolded, "You'd best get out of here, Billy D. McCann, before I set the dogs on ya'. Then you'll be sorry."

Ignoring her warning, Bill smiled beguilingly, his voice husky with emotion. "But friends should be friendly," he admonished, and held out his hand to her.

Without a moment's hesitation, Glory took it, happy tears glistening on her lashes as he pulled her into his arms. "And now that we're back together again, neither one of us will ever be sorry."

Epilogue

"What kind of speech do you call that?" Glory asked tartly as soon as her husband retreated from the podium and rejoined the family already seated at the picnic table. "Honestly, Bill, that effort was even worse than last year. You didn't even glance at the notes I prepared for you."

Bill winced at the well-deserved chastisement. "I'm sorry," he apologized sheepishly, knowing how hard Glory had worked to help improve his annual Fourth of July address to the townspeople. "It's just that standing up on that stage makes me so damned uncomfortable."

"Surely you could have endured the hardship for more than three sentences," Glory muttered with a frustrated shake of her head. "I can't imagine what folks are going to say."

"They're going to say that unlike our long-winded mayor, Bill McCann has a heart," Kenny supplied, popping a fluffy baking-powder biscuit into his mouth as he stood up to give Bill a hearty clap on the shoulder. "As far as I'm concerned, he done us right proud. He got up to announce this year's company dividend, stuck around long enough for folks to cheer the good news, then sat down like the kindhearted soul he is."

"Short and sweet," David asserted with an approving grin as he reached across the table to grab the last leg of fried chicken before Bill set his sights on it. "No man wants to listen to all that jawin' when he's tryin' to eat."

Zeke was quick to agree with his two brothers, though his appreciation for Bill's brevity had more to do with the growing wet spot on his jeans than any other reason. Striving to appear innocent of the problem, he handed the damp baby girl over to her father, then employed a strategic diversion. "A bit stingy on the salt pork this year, ain't ya, Aunt Ophelia?" he complained, taking a mouthful of baked beans.

Thoroughly offended by the unjust charge, Ophelia lifted the flat wooden spoon out of the large crock, showing off several thick slabs of meat. "I'll have you know, Ezekial Hubbard, that I fried up more'n a pound," she declared irately, then with deliberate malice, slung the sticky brown mass down on top of her errant nephew's glorified rice. "As you can rightly see!"

With a long-suffering sigh, Zeke leaned over his plate and continued eating, apparently pleased that his diversion had worked. By the time Bill discovered that his one-year-old daughter, Molly Lynn, was in drastic need of a new diaper, he was already seated at the head of the table opposite Glory. Holding the giggling blue-eyed baby in the air, he tried for a fierce scowl, but as usual when dealing with either of the red-headed twins, a besotted smile quickly replaced his disgruntled expression.

"Way to go, sweetheart," he chastised, giving the child a little toss that earned him another delighted giggle. "These were my best pair of white pants."

"I told you not to wear them this morning," his wife reminded him, then gasped. "Oh, no you don't, Merry Lee McCann!"

Needing both hands to keep their second rambunctious baby from crawling through a pan of barbecued ribs in order to get to her daddy, Glory used her foot to shove the diaper bag under the table in his direction. "At least you don't have cooked carrots smooshed in your hair and curdled milk running down your neck."

"Not yet," Bill agreed good-naturedly as he carried the diaper bag and his young daughter to the plaid blanket spread out on the grass next to the pavilion. "But the day's not over yet, is it, Molly, my girl?" he asked, as he lay the squirming baby down and efficiently disposed of the offending diaper.

Unfortunately he'd barely made it back to the table, intending to partake in the bountiful feast the sisters always prepared for the town picnic, when Jamie, who was surrounded by a large group of slightly older boys, hailed him from the head of the path leading to the baseball diamond. "Hurry up, Dad. I told the guys you'd pitch us some before the men take over the field."

"In a minute, Jamie," he called back. "I haven't even eaten yet."

This news was greeted by a disappointed, "But Dad! I promised," from his son and a lot of disgusted mumbling from his older teammates. Sensing that any further delay would ruin Jamie's chances for a tryout at the coveted first-base position, Bill sent one last longing look at Aunt Winnie's prize-winning fried chicken, then handed Molly over to Glory, who was already holding Merry Lee on her lap. As he reached under the table for his baseball glove, he heard her mutter something that he didn't dare ask her to repeat.

"Sorry, luv," he apologized, very much aware that he hadn't been making many points with his beloved wife all day and that he was about to lose a few more. "But what else can I do? The boy promised."

As if acting on some mysterious female instinct, Aunt Carrie came over and lifted one baby girl into her arms while Aunt Winnie picked up the other, giving Glory the chance to stand up and give her husband a proper dressing down. At least, that was what Bill was expecting her to do. Instead, after casting a last, lingering look at her own untouched plate, Glory slipped her arm through his and urged him to walk a little faster. "Let's go!"

"Go?"

"I swear you haven't listened to a thing I've said to you all morning," she scolded. "Those aren't just any boys Jamie's playing with, William McCann. They're the Dexster Street Dodgers, the team that won the Little League championship last year. They saw Jamie hit a few balls at the park yesterday and they said they'd be willing to give him a tryout. Once he shows them what a good job he can do in the field, they're bound to ask him to join the team. Wouldn't that be something?''

Bill grinned at the parental pride in her voice. ''Really something,'' he agreed, but he wasn't referring to his son's chances for joining the Dodgers.

''Hopefully, nobody will bunt,'' she continued worriedly. ''But if they do, you go in for it. We haven't devoted much time to that play yet, but we will. By next week, I guarantee, Jamie will be an expert at retrieving the short ball.''

Married for close to two years, Bill should have gotten used to it by now, but Glory's unconditional love for Jamie still amazed him at times. From the first, she'd treated his son as if he were her very own child, and it was obvious that Jamie loved her just as much in return. The boy's dark eyes positively lit up when he saw her, though his expression was anxious. ''Hey, Mom! Don't you have to be watchin' the babies?''

''The sisters are watching the girls so I can watch you. I wouldn't miss this for anything, Jamie McCann,'' Glory declared firmly, gesturing over her shoulder. ''The rest of the family will be here in a few minutes.''

Jamie looked past her, seeing that his uncles Zeke and David were already on their way across the square and a smile broke out from ear to ear. Turning around, he dashed exuberantly down the path, and the other boys quickly followed behind him. Before his wife could do the same, however, Bill wrapped one arm around her waist, dragged her up against him and kissed the daylights out of her. By the time he was finished, half the town was applauding his public display of affection.

"What on earth was that for!" Glory whispered, her face flaming with embarrassment.

"That's the way it works around here, L'il Bit," Bill replied unrepentantly, taking hold of her hand as he started down the path. "This kind of thing happens all the time to people who care so much about other people."

Glory tried to look furious, but her eyes were shimmering with a much more enduring emotion. "That's the way it works," she was forced to agree, since she'd once given him a similar reminder, but upon spying her husband's smug smile, she added tartly, "And don't you ever forget it, Billy D. McCann."

*   *   *   *   *

SILHOUETTE *Desire*™

COMING NEXT MONTH

#565 TIME ENOUGH FOR LOVE—Carole Buck
Career blazers Doug and Amy Hilliard were *just too busy*... until
they traded the big city winds for the cool country breezes and
discovered the heat of their rekindled passion.

#566 BABE IN THE WOODS—Jackie Merritt
When city-woman Eden Harcourt got stranded in a mountain
cabin with Devlin Stryker, she found him infuriating—
infuriatingly *sexy*! This cowboy was trouble from the word go!

#567 TAKE THE RISK—Susan Meier
Traditional Caitlin Petrunak wasn't ready to take chances with a
maverick like Michael Flannery. Could this handsome charmer
convince Caitlin to break out of her shell and risk all for love?

#568 MIXED MESSAGES—Linda Lael Miller
Famous journalist Mark Holbrook thought love and marriage
were yesterday's news. But newcomer Carly Barnett knew
better—and together they made sizzling headlines of their own!

#569 WRONG ADDRESS, RIGHT PLACE—Lass Small
Linda Parsons hated lies, and Mitch Roads had told her a
whopper. Could this rugged oilman argue his way out of the
predicament... or should he let love do all the talking?

#570 KISS ME KATE—Helen Myers
May's *Man of the Month* Giles Channing thought Southern belle
Kate Beaumont was just another spoiled brat. But beneath her
unmanageable exterior was a loving woman waiting to be tamed.

AVAILABLE NOW:

SILHOUETTE DESIRE™

presents

AUNT EUGENIA'S TREASURES
by CELESTE HAMILTON

Liz, Cassandra and Maggie are the honored recipients of Aunt Eugenia's heirloom jewels...but Eugenia knows the real prizes are the young women themselves. Read about Aunt Eugenia's quest to find them everlasting love. Each book shines on its own, but together, they're priceless!

Available in December:
THE DIAMOND'S SPARKLE (SD #537)

Altruistic Liz Patterson wants nothing to do with Nathan Hollister, but as the fast-lane PR man tells Liz, love is something he's willing to take *very* slowly.

Available in February:
RUBY FIRE (SD #549)

Impulsive Cassandra Martin returns from her travels... ready to rekindle the flame with the man she never forgot, Daniel O'Grady.

Available in April:
THE HIDDEN PEARL (SD #561)

Cautious Maggie O'Grady comes out of her shell...and glows in the precious warmth of love when brazen Jonah Pendleton moves in next door.

SILHOUETTE® Desire™

MAN OF THE MONTH

SCANDAL'S CHILD
ANN MAJOR

When passion and fate intertwine...

Garret Cagan and Noelle Martin had grown up together in the mysterious bayous of Louisiana. Fate had wrenched them apart, but now Noelle had returned. Garret was determined to resist her sensual allure, but he hadn't reckoned on his desire for the beautiful scandal's child.

Don't miss SCANDAL'S CHILD by Ann Major, Book Five in the Children of Destiny Series, available now at your favorite retail outlet.
